W9-AFF-044

# 259 Leaps,
# the Last Immortal

Other works by Alicia Kozameh

*Pasos bajo el agua* (1987, 2002)

*Steps Under Water* (1996)

*259 saltos, uno inmortal* (2001)

*Patas de avestruz* (2003)

*Ofrenda de propia piel* (2004)

# 259 Leaps,
# the Last Immortal

## Alicia Kozameh

Translated from the Spanish
by Clare E. Sullivan

Introduction by
Gwendolyn Díaz

*San Antonio, Texas*
*2007*

*259 Leaps, the Last Immortal*
© 2007 by Alicia Kozameh

Originally published as *259 saltos, uno inmortal*
by Narvaja Editor (Córdoba, Argentina)

Cover painting, "Fall" © 1997 by Andrea Belag
Courtesy of Mike Weiss Gallery, New York.

First Wings Press Edition

ISBN-10: 0-930324-87-0
ISBN-13: 978-0-930324-87-2
paperback original

Wings Press
627 E. Guenther
San Antonio, Texas 78210
Phone/fax: (210) 271-7805
On-line catalogue and ordering: www.wingspress.com
All Wings Press titles are distributed to the trade by
Independent Publishers Group
www.ipgbook.com

Library of Congress Cataloging-in-Publication Data

Kozameh, Alicia, 1953-
  [259 saltos, uno inmortal. English]
  259 Leaps, the Last Immortal / by Alicia Kozameh; translated from
the Spanish by Clare E. Sullivan; introduction by Gwendolyn Díaz.--
1st Wings Press ed.
      p. cm.
  ISBN 0-930324-87-0 (alk. paper)
  I. Title: 259 Leaps, the Last Immortal. II. Sullivan, Clare E., 1967-
III. Title.
  PQ7798.21.O9A135 2007
  863'.64--dc22

                                      2005033919

To the thousands of eyes that,
floating on their ultimate exile,
still give me light.

*And to Clare, Gwendolyn,*
*Bryce and Gustavo,*
*for all the effort.*

# A Portrait of Alicia Kozameh
# and Her Work

Alicia Kozameh is a dual soul, a woman of great strength and conviction, and a woman wounded by the turmoil she still carries within. She was born in 1953 in the city of Rosario, province of Santa Fe, in Argentina. Her father was a banker of Lebanese and Greek Orthodox origin. Her mother's family was Jewish, yet she converted to Catholicism in order to marry into her husband's family. Kozameh's older sister suffered brain damage at childbirth and was severely handicapped, a situation that placed a strain on the dynamics of the family.

Her father traveled from city to city working in various branches of the Banco de la Nación Argentina, which caused frequent changes in Kozameh's schools and surroundings. She attended Catholic high schools and when she was a student at Nuestra Señora de la Misericordia (Our Lady of Mercy) Kozameh helped to close down the school as part of the political rebellion called Rosariazo, a city-wide political demonstration against the government. This was in the late 1960s, a time of political unrest and violent outbreaks between the government and leftist activists.

After her sister died, Kozameh grew even more distant from her parents and left home at age seventeen. She lived in a boarding-house while studying at the Universidad Nacional de Rosario (National University of Rosario). At this time she also began her involvement with politics and activism, which led to a life-long search for justice and equality. In the early seventies, while she studied philosophy and literature at the university, she became a member of the PRT, or Partido Revolucionario de los Trabajadores (Workers' Revolutionary Party). Eventually, she was so involved in political activism that the PRT advised her to move to a different front within the party, lest she be arrested and possibly murdered, as so many others had been. She was apprehended by the police in 1975, shortly before the onset of the infamous "Dirty War" (late 1970s through the early 80s). While the overt intent of this regime was to purge the country of leftists, in fact what ensued was an era of repression and human rights abuses. After her arrest, Kozameh was kept in the sótano (basement) of the Rosario Police Station for fourteen months. After that experience, she was transferred to the prison of Villa Devoto, in Buenos Aires. Three years later – due mainly to pressure from groups like Amnesty International – she was released from prison. Because of a technicality (she had been registered in the police records when arrested), she did not suffer the fate of others who were said to have disappeared. The disappeared, or desaparecidos, as thousands of victims came to be known, were tortured and put to death by the repressive dictatorship that did not tolerate dissent.

Kozameh went into exile in California in 1980, where she took odd jobs such as house cleaning to survive. She had always felt the need to write and in California she made the time to write down her experiences. She published her first novel, *Pasos bajo el agua (Steps Under Water)*, in 1987. This work is based on the three years and three months that she spent imprisoned under the military dictatorship. Experimental in style, the novel is both political and personal. Throughout the work the victimized protagonist gradually rediscovers her own body and identity.

Her second novel, *Patas de avestruz*, written in 1989, was published first in German in 1992. The original Spanish version was published in 2003 in Argentina. This novel is based on the relationship between two sisters, one healthy and one incapacitated. Here, the author draws upon her experiences with her own sister to create a moving novel about love, hate and the frustration of living in a family marred by the distress of caring for a handicapped child.

In 2001 Kozameh published *259 saltos, uno immortal*. This English translation by Clare Sullivan captures the essence of the author's fragmented yet poetic vision. This work portrays Kozameh's experiences during her exile. It takes place in California and Mexico, where she lived after fleeing Argentina. In this novel she continues to experiment with style. Like a painting by Picasso, the work takes on meaning through its very fragmentary nature. It is written in sections ("leaps") that appear to be disconnected; however, there are threads of continuity that run through the book. Anecdotes, reflections, and characters are loosely woven together throughout the work, with the common denominator being the experience of exile, the feelings of estrangement, rupture and sadness, as well as the excitement of the new adventure. She names the novel "Leaps" because it reflects the emotional ups and downs experienced by people living in exile. This work is at once serious, playful and poetic. *259 Leaps, the Last Immortal* pushes the definition of novel into a new realm.

Many of Kozameh's stories have been published in anthologies and journals both in the Americas and in Europe. Among the more notable ones is "Bosquejo de alturas" ("Impression of Heights"), which takes place in a crowded basement of a police headquarters where a large group of women prisoners are being held. The story portrays both the fear and anxiety of their situation as well as the humorous coping strategies they devise to stay safe and entertained. It is a testament to the will to survive and to the power that friendship and solidarity can provide in the direst conditions.

*Ofrenda de propia piel* ("Offering of My Own Skin"), a collection of short narratives that continue to elaborate on themes of exile and enclosure, was published in 2004 in

Argentina. *Basse danse*, her fourth novel, will be published this year. In *Basse danse*, Kozameh, through the image of two very unique brothers, cultivates a metaphor of entrapment. She is currently working on her fifth novel with the working title of *Cantata*, about the experience of belonging to different types of groups. Here she continues to develop her interest in group psychology and loyalty.

Kozameh lives with her daughter, Sara, in Los Angeles, California, where she teaches Spanish language and creative writing. She speaks frequently in both political and literary conferences and remains actively involved with Amnesty International and other human rights organizations.

> – Gwendolyn Díaz, Ph.D.
> St. Mary's University
> San Antonio, Texas

# Translator's Preface

When I first began reading *259 saltos*, I was struck by its poetry. Indeed its form was reminiscent of a book of poems, complete with free verse-like prose and chapters as short as a few lines, even a few words. The writing itself I found to be almost musical, with words chosen as much for their "feel" as their meaning. During the translation process, I found myself reading most of the book's passages aloud, since their rhythm was carefully constructed and closely tied to the story line (a notable example being chapter 67 where the rhythm and repetition of "ascos que la acosan" [disgusting things that chase her] helps create a sense of pursuit). Complexities such as these frequently kept me from settling for simple, literal textual translations, as I strove, to as great an extent as possible, to retain their rhythms in the English version.

But of course the subtle interplay of rhythm and meaning was by no means the only difficulty posed by a work as complex as *259 saltos*. Sound was also a significant challenge (chapter 129 springs to mind here, as it is a paragraph composed entirely of 49 single words, all beginning with the prefix "des" – talk about getting to know your dictionary!).

Even so, what truly ties *259 saltos* so closely to poetry is the manner in which Kozameh relies on deeply convoluted, some might say nearly impenetrable, metaphor and imagery. Case in point, the eyes that confront the reader throughout the book. We find them peering out of the holes in plastic curlers, a synecdoche for disembodied Argentine political prisoners. Yet eyes also appear in other contexts, possessing other meanings: the eyes that progressively appear over the body of the narrator, for example, fluttering open and staring out, first from the back of her head, then her elbows, buttocks and belly. Are they pleading, judging, seeking to understand? Are they portals to another world, the new world of exile? As with so much poetry, the final determination lies with the reader, leaving the translator faced with age-old dilemma: how can I adequately translate a metaphor that I have only begun to grasp myself?

There are, of course, touchstones, most notably Argentine history and the author's own experience as a prisoner and exile. Her work, its images and emotions, can be placed within the context of the "Dirty War" and her subsequent travels to the United States and Mexico. Knowing this, one can imagine such a life, careening this way and that, almost absurdly, as if on roller skates. One can guess at the deep, personal meaning of a refrain like "cantar para no llorar" (singing to keep ourselves from crying) in the context of political persecution and torture. But of course in the end, one must realize one's own limits, both as a translator and fortunate soul.

I should make mention of the fact that for the first time in my career I've had the privilege and pleasure of working closely with an author. Our exchanges have allowed me to delve deeply into *259 saltos* and prize open many tough nuts. Such a collaboration was not without its perils, of course, as I frequently found myself adrift in the rough waters of the Spanish language. At times I had to fight to keep my head above the surface, to retain a distance from the material, and to keep my audience in view. For this I thank my husband Jim whose countless readings and questions kept me afloat. My colleagues at the University of Louisville, Mary Makris and Rhonda Buchanan, also helped me tremendously with their suggestions. And of course, my editor Bryce Milligan is responsible for bringing this novel to English-speaking readers. Thank you all.

– Clare Sullivan, Ph.D.
University of Louisville
Louisville, Kentucky

# 259 Leaps,
# the Last Immortal

*Hey, babe, take a walk on the wild side!*

– Lou Reed

**1** You absorb not quite half. Less. Much less. You manage to absorb a sixth of what happens. Your head, surrounded by a bright light, the bright light of Los Angeles, that doesn't quite blind you, that surrounds your temples but doesn't quite grab hold of them, your head deflects what's going on to the right and left, letting everything that won't be recovered escape into the shop windows along Santa Monica Boulevard. That first vision, the one that can never be recreated, fades as you move from place to place. The car moves forward and your brain dozes, confronted by the hunger of your naive, deluded eyes. What you didn't see today you won't see tomorrow. And there's no way to be tomorrow what you were today, and the sun's begun to set.

**2** It seems to go down red, reddened.

**3** Will you have to retreat, take one, two steps back, and take in the colors? Will you have to grant the new light control over the tones, over the various hues? Will you have to bestow on the new light the privilege of giving form to things?

**4** Or will you have to fight?

**5** This is Los Angeles: so wouldn't it be better to adopt a less warlike, more beach-friendly vernacular? Let's say: resist. Will you have to resist the image that the new light creates?

**6** The events contradict History. Appearing from two different corners, they advance in opposite directions with a cadence that makes me think they're on roller skates. And History, dumfounded, wonders what to do with them. Poor little History.

**7** Where to put them. How to distribute them. What tactic to use so as not to wound their sensibilities. So they don't get too worked up, too worried. So that in the midst of their nervousness their knees don't give out and they lose their balance and crash in a heap, decorating the sidewalk with gallons of bright, viscous red. So that all these events skating in direct opposition to History do not end up shattered  upon the parquet floor, the flagstones of the walkway, the grass of the plaza, the flowers of the Bel Air gardens, the sand of the beach.

And oh, pardon me, how forgetful: against the green shrillness of the hills of Hollywood.

**8** Ah, yes: against that green, green shrillness.

**9** And what if it were possible to find a way to put the brakes on little by little – true, first you'd have to clarify the meaning of "little by little," but okay – finally stopping them, oh, I don't know, with some little trick, a little white lie, by promising them a lollipop perhaps, or some chocolate treat, and then yes, not little by little but suddenly, pulling their skates out from under them, tearing them off, socks and all, and throwing them, so far they'll never find them again, and making them put on new shoes, stiff ones, so it's hard for them to walk, so it hurts, so they bleed, their feet breaking out in blisters, so they have to walk more slowly?

**10** Slowly?

**11** And what if, on top of their socks getting holes, they're left without socks? And what if on top of being left without socks or skates, the events up and have a fit of hysterics? And what if, instead of walking slowly due to their blistered feet, they decide, plain and simple, to stop walking?

And what if we're left without events?

And what if it occurred to someone that, given a choice between events that contradict History and a complete lack of events, the latter is preferable?

**12** Then what? Nothing reverberating against the green, green shrillness. Nothing against what sounds, smells like nothing. Bread upon bread, the food of fools, as they say in my country. You hear it from the lovers of contrast. Of the many, possible contrasts.

**13** It's under those circumstances that silence assumes its different forms, with the bread-upon-bread thing.

**14** But you've got to laugh. You've got to laugh a lot. A whole lot. Until you can't laugh anymore. You've got to be able to remember those moments of fearlessness, stretch your arms up to the sky – or up to the ceiling if you still believe in modesty – and flex your knees, and leap, hop around, stretch your belly, your waist, open your lips, show your teeth, open your throat and let loose an infinity of sounds. Or, why not, without stretching your arms to the sky, slowly settle your butt in whatever chair, airplane seat, park bench, sofa in your own house or your friend's or your lover's, close or half-close your eyes, breathe gently, smile gently, gently give a sigh. The kind that slips into the surrounding air from the corner of your mouth. Maybe the left corner.

There are so many ways to say yes to what we're capable of being.


**15**  It's under those circumstances that silence takes on its various forms: without the bread-upon-bread thing.


**16**  Without or with.
With or without.


**17**  You absorb a sixth. Or less. And even though Los Angeles is a city on wheels, no one's forcing you not to walk.

You go slowly, paying attention to the details. Because the details are really curious. Oh, the tall blond details, the ones with the braid and a "hi" face. Oh, the girls with the noses and lips of black people, but with blond, kinky hair, and green eyes. Oh, the Mexican gardeners and maids, waiting for the bus on the widest avenues of Beverly Hills. Oh, the black men and women on bicycles with curlers arranged just-so, determined to give their hair a good straightening. Ay, ay, ay, that tall black man with dreadlocks, so Rastafarian and beaming, a magnet for me, the one I gravitate to every time I approach the water (by car, of course) and walk along the boardwalk of Venice Beach. Oh, the details.

You go slowly, paying attention. Little by little a sixth becomes a fifth, a third, a half. Suddenly you manage to absorb half. Which isn't a little. Exile can cloud you over. Anesthetize you. Make you drowsy. Stupefy you. Really stupefy you: not in a figurative sense. No, no, nope: not in a figurative sense.

**18** Curlers. Curlers move me. As almost all the inhabitants of planet Earth know, curlers are now plastic. So that air can pass through to your hair, so your hair can dry, a plastic curler is full of holes. They vary in shape depending on the brand: some curlers are full of little round holes, others are full of little square holes. I don't know the limits of human imagination, so I don't know what each person imagines could be stuck, caught, embedded in each hole, square or round, of each curler on each head of the people who like to straighten or curl their hair. I do know, however, what I imagine: not a red piece of watermelon, not a green leaf from a tree, not an immaculate white key from a brand new piano, not a grayish piece of crumpled paper, written upon with blue ink and torn from some high school notebook and sent flying from some expert high schooler's hand. No. I imagine (and I even see him, I see him peeking out of the little round or square hole, looking tenderly into my eyes, watching me cross the busy Los Angeles streets, winking at me and giving me tons of courage and energy) an Argentine political prisoner. A man or woman prisoner. Surrounded by everyday things: a tin plate, a tin cup, a piece of soap, an abundance of cigarettes, some worn-out, clean underwear, a two-week-old letter from a five year-old son and, above all, more and more male and female prisoners. That more than anything: the rest of the Argentine political prisoners.

**19** You see them peeking out of the little holes in the curlers used by people who straighten or curl their hair. And you can also see them peeking out of all the other orifices that exist in this city. Which is the most spread out city in the world. All the holes: in the trunks of trees. In the clothes of the homeless. In the heads of crazy people. In the sewers where all the anguish pools up. You see them. Yes, you can see them.

**20** Seeing.

**21** Smelling.

**22** Not having an overly developed sense of smell leads, as we all know, to the development of other senses: very sharp vision, for example. You end up seeing everything. And there's the ever-increasing prospect of panoramic vision. Little by little, if you can believe it, you begin to discern different phenomena. Then suddenly, one day, there's an irritating sensation high up on the back of your neck, and you don't think much of it. But one or two days later it itches. It swells. Maybe it even hurts a little. Naturally you raise your hand to the spot and feel around, to find out what's happening. To the touch it seems to be something bulky and moist, and soft, despite the hair in the way. You rifle through your closets until you find a hand mirror and go to the bathroom, standing with your back to the bathroom mirror, which is big and faces the small one in your hand, and you brush away the hair from the troublesome area, and discover them: two marvelous eyes, similar to the originals you were born with, with long, arching eyelashes. Still closed, nevertheless. Surely they'll open tomorrow. The intensity of the surprise and the horror doesn't leave room for screaming. You remain as dumbfounded as History watching the events pass by on skates. As much or more. Your throat closes. Your knees seem overrun by an infinity of ants that, fortunately, are the kind that don't bite. Confusion causes the muscles in your hand to relax and the mirror falls to the floor and shatters. Hurry. Find another. There isn't one. Only the one in the little lipstick case. Let's see.

Look again. And, yes, there they are. With one small difference. The difference is that you perceive a kind of motion. It appears that the eyelids are trying to open now.

And your next thought is: what do I do? Should I cut my hair back there? Because, who on Earth would throw away an opportunity like this to see everything at the same time? But no, it's not necessary: at a touch, those locks of hair come loose. On their own. They fall, slipping past the shoulders, forming sinuous arabesques on the bathroom floor. And then, yes, the eyes begin to open up. Whoohoo!!! Hallelujah!!! They begin, yes they do, to open.

**23** They begin opening, opening. And, through the little mirror in the lipstick case, they even seem to shine with a smiling expression.

**24** But something got tangled between the entrance and the exit of my brain. Which are the same. The same door. That's what gets me excited: that the aperture for the entrance and the exit of our strokes of genius is the same. The collisions, the mixes, the concussions, the falls, the comings together, the battles, and the reconciliations among the uproarious, reckless crowd of ideas that enters and exits is what makes me love this white, weak and weighty ball. It's the source of my only happiness. Because your brain, I mean, come on, you've got to love it. Spoil it, understand it. Give it, every now and again, a little orgasm. Even a teeny tiny one, you know?

**25** That thing that snagged me: that question from a few pages back: Slowly?

**26** Slowly.
A word that usually generates deaf, blind, turbulent movements in my stomach muscles. But when that same word appears decorated with that elegant curling line and its pretty, sympathetic little point, before which everything becomes relative: that way, it doesn't make me sick to my stomach.

**27** Because it questions, but doesn't define. Because it doesn't define, but questions.

**28** Which is fine when it comes to that word but not for the ones that contradict it. Velocity, for example. And I, what the heck, why would I want to see it behind bars, coldly questioned?

**29** I want, really, with my entire being, to return to that aforementioned Slowly? But something's yanking me in another direction.

Because it's not easy to see, in spite of the brand new eyes on the back of my neck and everything that, yes, the rhythms change. And recognize it, let's not even pretend that it's easy to recognize it.

They change. They change. They change.

So that you don't hurt your body. So that your brain doesn't leap, doesn't scatter in fragments. So that, in the half-quiet of the purported observation, of the stare's so-called depth, the lungs relax and allow oxygen to enter. What oxygen? That stuff which, in combination with the usual mixture of who-knows-what, makes up the air of Los Angeles.

**30** With quite a bit of smog, certainly, in the mid-1980s.

**31** There are a variety of theories, ideas, conjectures concerning its origin, its functions, its level of importance. But for me a wristwatch is nothing more than a little circle, a little square, or a little oval of metal, or plastic, if we're going to consider only the most familiar versions of such passé kitsch, fastened to the wrist with a leather, or metal, or plastic strap, or any combination of those elements. Or others. I'm overcome with indifference to this kind of vanity. I'm guilty of other kinds of vanity, certainly, there's no one around here accusing me of modesty. But they simply bother me. They tickle the heel of my hand and that's serious. Nothing can nor should tickle my hand or anything near it. I want nothing in that area that would incite my writing hand to go on strike.

*11*

But a wall clock is another matter, something you simply can't ignore. If there's a table with twenty or thirty dinner guests sitting at it, all dressed in their most sophisticated attire, lace, silk and more lace, and a grand wall clock is hanging there in front of everybody, right in the middle of that majestic dining room. Who can resist watching and waiting for the exact moment when the long hand passes from one second to another?

Of course the transcendence of a moment like that is utterly destroyed by the desperation I feel when I'm confronted with one of those enthusiastic, energetic, unrelenting cuckoo clocks. Any old stick, a broom, kindling, whatever big spoon, skimmer, gigantic knife from whatever kitchen in the world, whichever Larousse dictionary, or Marion Webster's will serve to neutralize the noisy labors of that perky little bird, the one that won't peck at trees like the hardworking woodpecker, but that won't make the least bit of effort to restrain itself from pecking at my central nervous system.

## 32 Doot da-doo . . .

## 33 Or is it a grapefruit that's been injected with an overdose of hormones to accelerate its growth and which, at the end of the process, when it was large enough, was surprised by the appearance of some 700 steamrollers like the ones they use to flatten the ground before pouring pavement over it, which passed over it so many times that it was flattened flatter than a sheet of toilet paper, and maybe later the Indians, I mean some indigenous people, appeared, people who were lords and masters of the land until little old Columbus came along and showed his stuff, and they didn't get what happened to the Great Grapefruit God under

the steamrollers, and readying their arrows they let fly a few in an attempt to keep themselves from being conquered, arrows like watch hands, which for some reason didn't pierce the thing, but began to revolve around it instead? No. Let's not screw around here. It's only a wristwatch. Immense like a grapefruit pumped up with hormones. Immense like time. Projected backwards and forwards like facts and their consequences. Like the new facts that are produced with each consequence. The symmetry of the irretrievable.

**34** With the naiveté of a two month-old baby, in 1980, almost 1981, I wrote an ill-fated collection of words on a napkin of an LA restaurant, one of the cheap ones, a Denny's no doubt. Literarily lamentable. So much so that I ripped it up and mixed it with some leftover tomato sauce that I'd just choked down with some spaghetti, scraps that the elderly Mexican waiter carried off. Carried off forever.

And on the night of February 4th, 1999, at Teasers, while a certain close friend sang and pounded on the piano, bringing down the house with his southern rock band, I jotted down a literarily lamentable combination of words on a restaurant napkin.

Brian looked very serious up there belting it out, but his eyes spilled over to my table with intensity. Eyes that had traveled from Oklahoma City to Los Angeles leaving almost a whole lifetime behind.

*My name had been going away. Far away. In the distance they had been appearing: cement, the fluidity of air, the isolation of three or four stars placed who knows where now, in what density of silence, the newness of what is robbed of divinity by recently lived history, the form of the events that haven't happened, without having managed to decelerate, to stop as distance allows. The name of each one, of each one of us, had been placed far away, and had to be recovered. The task now was that recuperation, that passage toward rescue. A journey that should have been taken with open pores, when in reality all our pores were plugged by so much movement. And how to undo the obstruction? How to give the filter a good rinse? The rescue of a name was a fight that by necessity implied a victory. Any other option represented death. After which the question the facts demanded was: In what areas are we most alive. In what zones do we maintain healthy circulation. Where is that circulation most active. Something that had to be explored. And explored. And explored. And continued to be explored.*

And how important is it really to remember if this was written at the end of 1980 or the beginning of 1999, on a Denny's napkin or a Teaser's napkin? Alone, in 1980, in an attempt to eliminate some of the burdens of the everyday or, in 1999, surrounded by Brian and his band, my friend Liliana, and the inaudible music of ships rubbing against the nighttime surface of the water down by the marina?

**35** Carry the torches forward (David Viñas, an Argentine exile in Mexico, said again and again, as he smeared orange marmalade on an apple that he'd peeled and quartered for the two of us). Carry the torches forward, - (he used to say).

**36** And those of us who don't have torches?

**37** You absorb, you perceive, you grasp partially. The peripheral luminosity closes in. But it doesn't swallow up. Luminosity. So like the sea.

**38** A Greek guy. In his fifties. A widower. With a son about eight years old. With a fruit stand in a Glendale market. Or something like that.

**39** We'll remark upon it. We'll remember and remark upon it. And we'll leave it in writing.

**40** A Greek guy. A widower. With an eight-year-old son. In his fifties. With a fruit stand in a Glendale market. With a Greek-Spanish/Spanish-Greek dictionary tossed upon the patio table upon some heap of refuse. On a fake marble table, its legs invaded by the ocher acidity of rust. On the patio where he spent that confusing August. Although, who knows, as confusing as it was, maybe he wouldn't really agree. The next morning I would come to understand that he wasn't confused at all about his most intimate desires.

What was he showing Raúl and Marisa while the three of them toured the house and he spoke in that harsh and, for me, incomprehensible, English? What was he showing them? What was he taking out of the chest of drawers that faced the bed where I would be sleeping? What was it, besides what it actually was, that brown miniskirt, absolutely unforgettable and that I would never see again? What reason did Raúl and Marisa have for exchanging glances and avoiding my questioning look? They didn't have anything to say to me. What was the Greek, fifty-something widower, who needed help with the house, and who showed off the miniskirt categorically while he pointed at me, saying to them? What do you suppose that he supposed I had to do with that miniskirt?

How content I was those August nights of 1980 in Los Angeles! How sweet to have arrived without a cent, the ticket paid for by my circle of friends in Rosario who were trying to save my life. How splendid that the only option for work was serving a Greek widower, short but muscular. How refined, how delicate the brown-colored miniskirt was as it hung from the hands of my brand new boss. How harmonious Marisa and Raúl were as they left in their Audi telling me that everything would be fine, that there are only two bathrooms to scrub, so I should focus my attention on the boy, since I like children so much and am sympathetic to people with family drama. How inspirational the speech that Marisa gave as the Audi pulled away: You see, for tried and true revolutionaries like us, life gives us a chance to sacrifice ourselves even in Los Angeles, to prove our nerves of steel to the world. Of course. Even in L.A., *che*.

And one absorbs half. Less, really. Less than half.


**41** It doesn't matter what you are. At times it doesn't matter what the thoughts, the desires that chase us, hound us, are. You bleed yourself dry trying to figure out, for example, what others expect of you. What others are thinking about your appearance, about the look in your eye, about the surprise that becomes evident, that becomes entangled with your features, that surprise with which you greet what's happening around you. What will others think your needs are, your desires. The horrifying chasm that always exists between our own impressions of people and the beliefs they nurture about themselves can leave you slack-jawed, completely defenseless. Between our profound, indubitable understandings and those of others.

Doot da-doo . . .


**42** It's almost like having swallowed a hundred trays of ice cubes without melting or crushing them. As if the ice had been hammered down your half-closed throat. Icy cold, stiff with blood pulsing crazily against a heart with no way out, you walk from the front door after saying good-bye to your friends, say good night to the Greek guy and his son, enter the assigned bedroom, lock the door from the inside with two turns of the key or whatever it took to safeguard the house in that moment of U.S. History, and wait for the night to transpire. Without undoing even a button, without taking off your shoes, without mussing the bed or covering yourself with the sheets. Ready for whatever might occur. Ready for the succession of seconds marked by the clock that was going to wake me up at six in the morning, in the improbable event that my eyelids would ever meet each other. Ready not to let the tears invade me, weigh me down: it wouldn't be advisable for me to be serving breakfast to the boy with puffy eyes.

Ready to tighten, yes, yes, to tighten, to compress the thoughts, the explosion of moving forms entering through my temple, carrying out their carnivalesque dance, beating against my cranium, and sliding among the fissures and the furrows of my brain, my soft, slobbery brain. Ready to keep them from slipping out my other temple. The forms and images, Maura, old and tough Maura, Maura the fighter. Silvana hoarse from the effort of teaching her secret first aid class in a low kind of voice, inaudible to the jailer from, oh why not go ahead and say it, Japan. Griselda's forehead lined and cold from having spent too much time leaning against the metal upright of the prison bunk. Tighten, compress, tighten the succession of colors and movements, of silences and anxieties, while my political exile's muscles in their new job of housemaid can't find a way to define their desires, their necessities, their urgencies. And in the meantime I won't allow even one of those ticking seconds to pass without being counted, released from the semi-luminous sphere, in their march toward six o'clock in the morning . . .

**43** . . . and in the meantime my muscles won't act like muscles, won't keep me weighed down on the dark, Matelasse bedspread. Me, the levitator, the Levitator of Glendale. And in the meantime I ask myself the reason for my own name. For my own existence. And in the meantime I interrogate myself about the possible effects of the sound of my name, of each one of the letters that comprise it, in the event I should decide to shout it out, against the air. Now, as in el Sótano: with my shoes tied tight, no matter what. And as I've said before: the clothing that covers me. Always on.

**44** And, yes. That's how progress happens, a little in one direction, a little in another, the course of what we call life. Looking over here, spinning our head over there, twisting our neck too far forward. Straining our shoulder blades so they'll allow us to glance back at what we've left behind us. Those things that stick to our shoulders, in our eyes, like gum, like tar on the bottom of our feet, between our toes, at the edge of the beach.

**45** But before life could progress any further, really, in my case morning arrived. The alarm didn't ring at six because it would have been an unnecessary noise. I'd kept watch, like in el Sótano, but for more than the usual two hours and without the consolation of a *compañera* to communicate with in a quiet, muffled voice. No, no, no. Besides someone was about to knock on my door, and I wasn't the least bit prepared for that eventuality. The tiny voice of a child tinged with early-morning hunger was saying, urgently and plaintively, mama, mama, I want my breakfast.

I opened the door quickly, very quickly. I opened the door and faced him. And let loose my awful, brazen English to demand who it was that had told him that I was his mother. And he understood me, yes, I swear to God, cross my heart: he understood me. He answered that he knew I wasn't his mother, but that he also knew that I would be soon. Put that in your pipe and smoke it, you who don't believe in magic. You skeptics, you who don't believe in miracles and such things. I understood him. And he understood me.

I left the bedroom following that already squat (though not yet muscular) figure. He walked me to the kitchen and showed me how to pour cereal into a dish. Evidently the boy sensed a kind of ignorance in me that he couldn't identify. And since his doubts clearly pertained to how to make him breakfast, he decided to instruct me with great tact and poise. In other words it was he who did it, slowly, deliberately, and unerringly: without dropping a single cereal flake or spilling a drop of milk. And while the little boy demonstrated his meticulous and perfection-ist nature, the father's Greek head suddenly popped through the door that connected the patio to the kitchen, the father, who'd left for work at daybreak and who, for who knows what reason, chose to show up at that very moment . . .

**46** . . . because I was the one who was supposed to be in charge of the house. In charge of cleaning and of caring for the house and the boy while the father, the small but muscular Greek, was away. I had supposed he'd be away from four in the morning until seven in the evening, at a minimum.

**47** Presence. Opposites. Absence. Forces exercising pressure against each other, and the tempests: Who can really say, can recognize, the difference between being present and being absent? What is it to be and what is it not to be? Who is and who is not? What is it to have been and to have ceased to be? What is it to have really been, with your whole, present body, in the day-to-day struggle, in search of a detail, of an idea, of a way to go about creating a more beautiful scheme in which to contain the dimensions of this world? What is it to have stopped being what one once was, what one had done? What is it to have been part of the form and the contents, and to have stopped being so?

Who was and who is no longer? Who were and who are no longer? How many were and how many no longer are? Where are those who were before and who suddenly stopped being?

**48** Be warned. He who asks should be prepared for a bitter answer.

**49** And so the first question, implicit in the tone of the narrative, is: why does the Greek gentleman, the greengrocer from the Glendale market show up at his house at this very moment?

**50** And you'll have to root out the answer from wherever it was attempting to hide. From wherever it was that it was tricking you with mimicry. You'll have to go along reloading it, since between one volley and another, its outlines get a little discombobulated. And you'll have to reorganize it if, in the effort, its elements get rearranged. And you'll have to write it down and leave it stationed in a secure zone, perhaps conspicuously. In case we, the living, decide to become amnesiacs. So that we're obliged to take a look at it once in a while through the wateriest corner of our eye, even though it seems the least interesting, the least active vantage point.

**51** He came into the kitchen through the patio door, and ordered his well-schooled son (this scenario had already been played out several times before with a series of co-protagonists) to take his bowl of cereal and milk to his room and eat it there, with the door tightly shut. An order that the boy, in his proverbial wisdom and discipline, followed without a word. And I saw, like a bolt of lightning, the compactness and vigor of the Greek leap upon me. With his tense muscular hands grabbing my tense and not so muscular tits. Boom. Against the refrigerator. Which shook violently. As a way of complaining, I suppose. Since the situation was worth complaining about. The poor little innocent unsuspecting refrigerator, whose only desire and function in the midst of this muddy heap of events (which were not merely on roller skates, but bearing down like Fittipaldi's Formula 1) was to work, to do what was asked of it, to make that continuous little muffled sound at certain intervals, and, incidentally, keep the fresh and the cooked food at a steady temperature to prevent it from rotting.

Putrefying, you might say. You know, in order to do justice to the semantic properties of the obliging word. So that the word might fully exercise its virtues. So that it might tell all. So as to avoid hurting its feelings. So that it wouldn't feel disdained. So as to carry out its function of parable, simile, allegory. A veracious representative of what it designates and describes. With integrity.

**52** And why wouldn't Mr. Greek greengrocer not attempt to hook up with the faithful and reliable refrigerator (that, by the way, wasn't going to let loose bothersome shrieks that would drive him like a shot back to his produce stand, that wasn't going to pick up the phone and disclose, breathless and seized by terror, to her friends who had dropped her there the night before, those things that she wasn't ready to believe, demanding that they rescue her from the horror this instant, this instant) instead of employing servants and trying to rape them? Though refrigerators do have tiny wheels down below. Don't they? And, who knows, under the right circumstances, you know, with the proper motivation, given no other choice, your guess is as good as mine, they might even manage I don't know what. But I don't know what I'm trying to say, and this is no time to fool around.

**53** And, speaking of presences and absences, we now witness the refrigerator, white, enormous, angular and more excited than usual, fresh, cold, with frozen insides full of many-colored, many-flavored foods, apparently never weighed down by the monotony of its job of preserving, unassuming on the outside and with a certain irregular texture, rigid and hard and definitely quadrangular, we witness it in motion. Now running haphazardly toward the front door, dragging the bag that contained clothes and books to last six days, opening the door, slamming it behind her, and halting at the corner, at a Glendale intersection, supposedly, to await in a state of agitation, the arrival of her friends' Audi which, after dropping her into that incomprehensible hellhole the night before, now, at seven o'clock the following morning, had no choice but to come and get her.

Surrealism, Postmodernism, Dadaism, the Latin American Boom, turn of the century, pastiche, Cold War, boiling war. Who really cares?

**54** And you, kid, what's with you? Can you bring yourself to face these relatively wild forms? Because I mean, let's not even mention their contents. Let's not raise them. Shhhh, quiet as mice. Don't wake them, don't disturb the crazy contents. They could ruin our peace. Our happiness. Our existence.

**55** Shhhh.

**56** But, uh, what is a content? What is it, how do you delineate it, what does it represent, how do you look a content in the face? An itty bitty content. Not pretending to be more than it is. A sorta-kinda content. A content in progress. A big ol' honkin' content? Or a concentrated content. A nucleus. An essence. A substance. A blood spot on an egg.

**57** But it needn't be a question of thinking about it too much. Since no one is master of the definitive thought. As it is, your most original ideas appear and are forgotten, or are discarded as useless, in the same way you turn on or turn off a lamp in some corner of your house. And precisely because the monopolizers, devourers and appropriators of the last word multiply like rabbits as they fight to impose a point of view, we know that no one is master of the last word. So meditation, reconsideration, reconstruction of the whole series of approaches to the subject, interrogation, I don't know, it remains to be seen. It's a simple matter of competence, know what I mean? Everything seems to revolve around whoever it is that has the nerve, to either speak or jot down on paper, to greater or better effect, the occurrences so that they may one day be of modest help, or maybe not, in giving a believable form, for their comprehension, to the facts as we have lived them, whether in the footsteps of a man, a woman, a cat, at a run, on a motorcycle, on a train, without taking a single step, sometimes without rhythm, in time with enchanting melodies, or in long strides, or stumbling along, or in leaps.

**58** Content (fuck!) is a thorn stuck between the dermis and the epidermis of the tip of the right pinky, since it's not worth ruining your index finger, for example, or your thumb, seeing as how life demands that you survive, with an intangible point, but one that can be imagined nonetheless. It's that little thorn, so wise in its form, underscoring the sharpness of one of its ends, yes, of course, alive, long live life, long live action, long live liberty, long live the sharpness of the end and long live the growing variations of the sharpness. That form, rather squared at the base, offering us a kind of reassurance, where everything is simplified, flattened, and luke-warmed. What a brilliant vision, that thorn's essential reality, the combination of a reliable base and a penetrating point. Penetrator. And again penetrating.

So much so that it knows how to remain still after having staked its claim, so rooted in that it stays there, irremovable, with that attitude it has, a little defiant, a little circumspect, almost so you kind of fall in love with it, the little manipulator, playing so meek and defenseless, like I just need a little room, and working its way in, being careful not to move either this way or that, not causing the slightest sensation, quite something, don't you think? Not it, no, snug in its comfy little hole, so quiet, yet so adamant that you not forget it. And on top of everything, desperate to survive. But by what means? What cunning will it employ to achieve its aims?

I wonder. Will it eat? Will it nibble a finger? Will it absorb the cells of the hair follicles, of the sweat glands, will it join the excreting function of the skin, sipping some of the sweat, of the fatty tissue, and of the urea? Will it consume some part of the epidermal walls, those that it fought for and managed to take some permanent refuge in?

Oh, my sweet, the contents. Oh, precious one, the things that are created on the inside. Oh, my dear, the things that develop and grow monstrously in our guts. Oh, oh, those things we contain, and oh, those things that contain us, those things that keep us contained, those things that dare to contain us, that defy us to be who we are, that won't allow us to be anything else, that celebrate what we believe ourselves to be. Oh, my darling, so many bruises, so many caresses, so many little critters (and these things are wriggling), so many sweet, pretty little bugs, the tickles that spill into my bloodstream and keep me awake, half-asleep, oh, love of my life, the contents, your contents, I'm sleepy, I'm sleepy, a kind of drowsiness overcomes me (attacks me), and I'm going to take a nap, a short nap, don't get frightened, just enough to recover my energy.

 Slight smile. Tenuous laughter. A weightless cackle. Ha. Ha.

**60** I'm not going to say that it's to keep from crying, because I mean, why. Even though, in reality, a really good laugh, one you'd consider hearty, also deserves a few tears here and there. So, by that reasoning, if you let loose tears when you laugh as well as when you cry, it's the same thing. Right? Because, in that case, what's the damn difference?

It's like my cousin whose name I can never remember, who always has, or had as a girl, this fat, chubby face, all red, the idiot, her eyes down, always looking down, and her chin stuck in her chest. Embedded. And her hair like a curtain, impossible to tell if she was walking forward or backward, advancing or retreating, so much hair in her face. So flushed that fat face that you could never tell if she was crying or laughing. When our gang of cousins would romp around the gray and sickly patio at the house of the grandmother we barely knew, and one of us would play a joke and the rest burst out in yellowish, greenish laughter, we'd think she was crying. The mystery always remained spinning in the patio air above our heads. And when someone whacked his knee on the terrible tiles of the floor and silence fell on everyone with the convulsive crying of the injured one, you could hear what we thought was an infectious laugh, also a bit convulsive, emitted from her puffy and amorphous cheeks, or from some orifice that she must have had between one reddened cheek and the other. And, considering your perspective, it was the same. Right? What did it matter if chubby cheeks laughed or cried? Who the hell was chubby cheeks anyway? And why was I going to have to remember her name in the future? What difference is there between laughing and crying?

What is laughing? And crying? And what do we want to accomplish with so much weeping? And with so much rejoicing: after all we've been through, I'm asking in all seriousness, with our history, how can we rejoice?

**61** My neighbor talked about it every so often, the journalist, who heard it from his friend's mother, who, for her part, heard it from the schoolteacher she used to run into at the beauty salon.

**62** Just so there's no confusion. Because I mean who wants to have a cousin, or admit you have one, with cheeks so big you can't tell if she's laughing or crying? Not me, for one. Better to put her in a remote spot, conveniently lost with respect to our existence in the world.

**63** And with the wind that pounds, that beats us. That sticks to us. That disgraceful wind, oh my love, that buffets us, leaving us stranded in sobs.

**64** But no, doesn't drag us away.

**65** But the softness, but the solidity, but the liquidity, but the fluidity of your superhuman body.

**66** Of your extraordinary body. Stupendous. Maybe that way we can convince her. By praising her. By telling her how beautiful she is. By highlighting all her potential. By making plain, and thereby making her see, all her wonders. By pointing out her perfect posture. Her own, unexpected sinuous curves. Her subtleties, and those, shall we say, entertaining detours that her madness takes every so often.

Because boring, she sure doesn't bore anyone. Which is worth considering. So outgoing, so full of audacity and heroism, so surprising in each decision she makes. Let's see if we can't convince her. Let's see if we can't make her understand that we need her, that she's indispensable to us. So knowing. Such a magician. With her long tubular black dresses that leave only her shoulders and ankles exposed. The softness, the solidity of your dimensions. Of your superhuman body.

Always so ready to deploy her resources, her strategies. So elusive. Let's see if we can calm her, let's see if we can't convince her to modify some of her rhythms. It would be better if she didn't pass by us that way, playing the distracted one, without even looking. Because the truth is that she doesn't even have to look for us. We're right there, on the lookout for her every move. Her whims. So she might wait for us. So she won't disappear on us slipping between Earth and sky at such velocity, via that line that doesn't exist and that some call the horizon. So History might wait for us. So she might wait.

**67** So she might wait for us attentively, with antennae up and alert, with pores open or in the promising process of opening. With the aged, dried out, sluffed off cells being released into the space they'll soon occupy in the air, and freeing the orifices so they might breathe.

So History might wait for us. Seated on her throne of rubies, encrusted in the white gold of will and patience. Or peering out of the most overflowing garbage can in the most distressing neighborhood in this world. From iniquity. From perversity. From her corner of desires. It doesn't matter from where. Because in the end everything gets here. Because in then end things happen one day.

So she might wait for us. With all the active cells of

her flesh and her bones, molecules in their rubbing
motion, in rhythms that keep her senses alert. So she
might perform a few gymnastics every so often. So she
might purge her toxins. So she might let loose the nausea
that's stalking her. So she might wait.

Dancing. So she might wait, dancing a waltz. A min-
uet. Or rock from the 70s. Yes. There's no doubt. Better
a rock 'n' roll tune, where you don't need to have a dance
partner. Where you can be detached, elevated, without
someone else's hands on your waist. So she might wait,
dancing to rock and roll with musical violence and naive
wisdom. So she might wait a while to finish her dance
before she starts to run amuck, crazed.

**68** Because that compañero who had been left
locked in a cell in a jail for political prisoners
in some part of the southernmost country in
the world, still doesn't arrive. He doesn't arrive, still.
Even though he still has those gray-blond curls.
Somewhere. Inside that scalp, shaved clean. Or almost.
They are, supposedly, potentialities, compressed springs
that will eventually leap forth. Perhaps those whitened
shadows are going to surface again, to take, if not a form,
what might be called the idea of a form. That will be sufficient to sustain the electric currents in the body and in
its yearnings, in the length of the hair and in the conscience, in the contours of the waist when reclining in
your favorite armchair and in the frequency with which
you wash your navel, in the rhythm of your hips in
motion and in the last thought before dying, those currents that we will not allow to travel backwards as if into
the past.

Such that in that way, more or less in that way, practically without a sound, you can let loose a sort of . . .
Doot da-doo da-doo. . . *Hey, honey, take a walk on the*

*wild side* . . . before we become excessively serious and arrogant and begin to teach the world about that thing we call exile:

That hat. That pebble that got stuck in your shoe. The peeling bark of that tree. That green t-shirt that looks so bad with my olive skin. That book we read again and again. And in that book, the page that makes us remember most that we're alive. The hidden significance of the knots in the wood of that table. That ceramic ash-tray where ashes are replaced with our meager collection of silver earrings. That shout to one's own child. That suf-focating embrace of one's own child. That coffee that accompanies the first version of a text. Those Mexican papayas. Chilean grapes. Argentine pears. The arrival of summer in California, when the imported fruit concedes its place to the local variety: recognizing the difference. That genuine desire to walk along Venice Beach and the real possibility of doing so. The windy sky of April. The sunny sky of July. That new mole discovered in a recent-ly shaved armpit. Those disproportionate rages. That tight, black velvet skirt that, thanks to a tiny amount of spandex, fits well enough to let us feel in our stomach, in our elbows, a sort of transparent happiness. That idea of having learned to observe everything fixing one eye on the mouth of the person you're speaking to and the other on the moving picture of our history. That street. Every street.

But he still doesn't arrive, and the anxiety gets spun, the threads of the imagination come together, then get poured into molds, then shaken, then stirred with the intensity of a cocktail, the threads and the knots get whipped into a cocktail, because if we want a cocktail well then we'll sure as hell have one, and when we empty the whole thing on the table top so we can see how tangled it is, he'll appear before our eyes (the ones in our head and the ones that appeared not long ago on our neck) that curly-headed blond who you were in that corner bar one afternoon in 1973 near the School of Arts and Sciences in Rosario between classes. We'll see him grow and move around. And speak. And use all his powers of persuasion to convince us that life without him is a complete waste of time. We'll hear him expound on the benefits of breaking up with the old boyfriend, an architect (or about to be one), something we would have done anyway, if only because we knew one day we were going to have to listen to a speech like this, and the benefits that will accrue as a consequence, like for example renting a place, an apartment, an old house, a shack out in the country, it doesn't matter, and together building a golden bridge to happiness, "a word which, from this point forward, can't exist, because while there is one unhappy person in this world, it is impossible to be happy", an idea, words, with which we were in complete agreement at that moment, at that moment, and afterwards, and always, because for some people there's no other way to conceive of one's own existence.

We will see him grow and move around and speak to us and convince us and we will see ourselves completely and maybe for the first time truly in love. And your big blue eyes, ferociously staring, poised for attack, will attack. Because the organs of the body must do what they were made to do: We can't allow them to weaken with idleness. They will attack and they will win the battle that's already been won.

And six years later we'll see him descend from an Aerolíneas Argentinas airplane in the Los Angeles airport surrounded by a large grayish storm cloud, a curious mix of machismo and unease, that won't precisely awaken my desire to make love to you. That will no longer awaken my desire to make love to you. Or to let you make it to me. Or to make it at all. Not in exile.

But that, that fragment of the heroic deed, comes later.

Even if, I don't know, prematurely, I have to say it: something, something in that face, is different. Something in that face.

**69** You go along absorbing a part. A larger part.

**70** One would suppose that watches should keep time. Times. One would suppose that the hands should revolve, clinging to the passage of time with the anxiety of a boyfriend sick with jealousy. With the fidelity of a mother who's seen her son disappear at the hands of a group of Argentine police, in the midst of the confusion of machine guns and bare-fisted blows, and who will dedicate what remains of her energy to searching for him. One would suppose that the watch hands will be completely devoted to the designs and the perfections of a faultless Swiss machine, because marking the passage of time should be a faultless activity. Always in sync. Shouldn't it?

But then, what do the watches do and what do the watch hands do, and what do the watchmakers do, and what do their owners do, if time decides to take a break from all that running? If it needs a siesta, I mean.

**71** Can you picture all kinds of watches piled up in mountainous heaps full of brilliance and reflection, tick-tocks and cuckoos, mounded in an immense mass grave, practically the size of the planet? Because I mean there used to be, there were, once, back when it was necessary to calculate the passage of minutes, so many watches. There were so many. Can you picture them?

**72** I. You picture the accumulation of watches. The eyeglasses. The shoes. The gold teeth. The relapses. The circularity, the shameless-ness of time's impertinent nature, to stretch and wad like chewing gum, until it makes you nauseous.

**73** The idea doesn't make me the least bit afraid, the least bit anxious. On the contrary. That a watch would work faultlessly is a real prob-lem. Because so often guilt overrides your compulsive desire to open it, take it apart, and examine its guts. So you can put in new and different mechanisms that you invented yourself. So you can tinker, maybe with a nail, wedging it between one little wheel and another. So you can pull the beautiful little golden wheels off of the even more beautiful cogs and find other things to do with them: stick them to a painting made of different little pieces of metal, find a strong thread for them and make them into a necklace that you'd have to find a black dress for, or delicately place them on a dark little dish so you can enjoy looking at them again and again. Whatever.

**74** Fearful that time is not passing, no. I'm not. If only we were able to wake up this morning and discover it were still yesterday. Magnificent. We would make other arrangements. We would count how many *compañeros* are active, and not how many have been, are being, assassinated.

**75** And so continues the process of feeling out new spaces. What is she thinking – in English, of course - that tall and very blond woman with blue eyes, regal bearing and the attendant

33

dignity of a queen spread all over her body, as she watches me ponder how I'm going to clean the enormous windows of her Pasadena mansion with any effectiveness? Crossing the living room, my *patrona* glances around. Then after two or three minutes she crosses back again and takes another look. And there's me, trying. Honestly. Squeezing the trigger on a bottle of her favorite brand of cleaning liquid and rubbing the window with balled-up newspapers. Pretending to know how. Or maybe knowing already. And she, never taken by surprise, approaching finally. Advancing with an enormous Spanish-English and vice-versa dictionary. Shit, she wants to talk. She invites me to leave the window cleaner and the balled-up papers on the polished wood floor and to be seated in one of her ample armchairs, facing her, already seated with her enormous dictionary. And I hear: Dear, my dear. I am a little worried. I have the impression that this house, with its six bathrooms and large number of bedrooms, sitting rooms, the enormous kitchen, the two floors, the basement and attic, is too much for you. Last week, after the interview that we had to get to know each other, my husband said to me, "And this girl, with those hands, what do you think she is going to clean?" And I answered him: possibly nothing. But I want her with me. I am going to ask her to put the library in order. But you insist on cleaning, and there is something that does not fit with all this. You are not Mexican, but you do not speak English well. You do not know how to clean a house, you seem educated, but you are working as a live-in servant. What is going on? Who are you?

The dictionary had been employed repeatedly over the course of that little paragraph, and the fibers of my throat became increasingly entangled with every word I managed to understand. And even though I objectively knew that in my new life as a political exile there was no reason to hide the truth, or almost none, I opted for self-censorship. And so my blood pressure dropped. So much so that my mistress, the elegant lady of that impressive Pasadena mansion, led me tenderly up the carpeted staircase to my room, her arm around my waist, and put me to bed, covered me, gave me a kiss on the cheek and closed the door behind her.

**76** And closed the door behind her.

**77** And opened it again one hour later. To see how things were going. I was awake, face down, with my right arm dangling toward the floor, where I had a notebook open and was writing. A poem. Yes: a poem. She noticed the form and asked: Do you always write poetry? A nod of my head answered in the affirmative. But I leapt from the bed, got dressed, and ran to continue with the enormous windows, with the crumpled paper and her favorite brand of cleaning liquid.

And at dinner my sole job was to sit at the table with my mistress' husband, in other words my *patrón*, and one of their four children, who, in spite of being 25 and old enough to pay rent, still occupied a room in her parents' house. This as the lady of the house served us all a meal that she'd spent a considerable number of hours preparing. And while the four of us were chewing this frugal, discreet, noiseless, tense supper, a sound rose amid the tinkling of the silverware and the sound of fresh lettuce leaves being torn between our teeth: Tell us why you came to the United States. It was the same voice from a few hours before. And while the three of them awaited an answer my *patrón*, in a noble gesture of support to his life partner, stretched and grasped the huge dictionary. The one that moved around the house according to the requirements of my ignorance, and theirs. The all-powerful dictionary. And he gave it to me with a dentist's smile. I am a political exile, I managed to say between the pieces of celery and avocado (*palta, aguacate*) still slipping around in my mouth. And I let loose: about the Argentine situation, about activist groups, about justice, about poverty. About repression. And I went on at length about that, given that I knew so much. I said that I was a writer and a Liberal Arts student, that they razed the house where I lived with my *compañero* (without adding details about his tempestuous blue eyes and diabolical, ashen curls), that I was a prisoner for several years, that he was still in jail and so on and so forth. And when I was more or less getting to the part where I was boarding the plane toward exile in Los Angeles, when the creaky pages of the all-powerful dictionary began to seem light from so much handling, I raised my blinking eyes to produce the final effect, but it wasn't necessary: Everyone, all three members of the family for whom I was performing the role of servant, were crying inconsolably. Inconsolably. And they stood and came around the table toward me and embraced me and kissed me and said things like consider yourself part of the family, now we have five children, we'll help you in whatever way you need. And no one was eating anymore. And no one finished eating.

**78** And the next morning my *patrona* added an ample desk to my furnishings. And on the desk, smiling, showing off a multitude of orderly, gleaming teeth, an electric typewriter. And in my bathroom a lot, I mean a lot, of very white, creamy bars of soap. They were enough, each one, if I were lucky, for two sumptuous showers. In my sumptuous bathroom.

**79** I say to you, without agonizing over it too much (and without forgetting to use each and every one of your abilities to observe in detail what's around you): take a walk. Always being careful to adjust your rhythm as new things pop into your field of vision. Always keeping in mind that you are a transplanted blossom, a wisp of cloud lost in someone else's skies, a slice of plantain swimming in the tomato sauce of a huge, meaty rice stew. Got it? You following me?

**80** And then, not long after, the elections. And my mistress fought with her whole family convincing the children to vote for Carter. And even so, she had to punish her husband with a month-long silence because, naturally, he voted for Reagan. He endured insults. And different arguments. The most persuasive of which was: How could you vote for that disgrace of a man? After what people like him did to this girl (me) and her friends, you heard it from her yourself. How could you? A month without a single word. Some of the children also joined in these drastic measures (against the irreversible). And the man slunk around. He dragged his feet around the immensity of his own mansion. He dragged his hands around his dental practice, he dragged his Mercedes along the Los Angeles highways, he dragged his humanity through his own history. Until he asked for forgiveness, and received it. You see this phenomenon in Southern California all the time, don't you? I saw it time and time again in those days: forgiveness, second or third or fourth chances, the abiding freedom to change one's mind (because of course it's the land of freedom) at any moment and under any circumstance, forgetfulness, or some other weakness of the heart or mind. And, who knows, probably also in Northern California, and in the North, and on the East Coast, and in the rest of the West, and in the rest of the South, and ultimately, in the lower strata from which this country grows, upon which it rests, and in the vast blue sky, the lid of the great frying pan in which its citizens are frying little by little.

**81** Now don't shout, don't you shout. All you who think that the end of the 20<sup>th</sup> century means the end of hope and the end of utopia, the end of yearning for a more just world, and the end of Marxism, think again, *che.* Look at what I actually said: I didn't say that they are already fried. I said they are being fried. Little by little. That's what I said: that they are being fried.

**82** You have to be able to speak your mind. You have to be capable of saying it all. To the man who at twenty had shaken our every cell, who had been sufficiently resounding, colorful, hyperactive, entertaining, and clear-headed, who had not asked permission to reach out and place his hand between our legs, who had known exactly how, how, who had insisted on sharing a little house whose bathroom was a hole in the middle of the bare earth, twenty meters away, all so he could work in a nearby factory whose workers suspected that they would only find respite from their peculiar pains by fighting to eliminate them, who was less fearful than they say is necessary, whose Lee blue jeans showed off his perfect ass, who was so insistent about certain issues (like for example that the whole life of a revolutionary – like him, I guess – should be revolutionary) until it became increasingly difficult to swallow his story, the sweet, exalted, arrogant, naïve, insecure, emotional, deceitful, starry-eyed, generous one, the one capable of bringing incalculable histrionic energies to bear merely to impress, the intense one, the worried and at times a little bit saddened one, you had to keep loving him.

**83** Even after leaving jail. In exile. Even afterwards. And forever.

**84** Well, yes, some used to say, but anything stuck together with snot eventually comes unstuck. It's that simple. And it was understood. Of course. Ultimately, the supposed thing had to be glued with something more effective. Less natural. More synthetic. More reliable. Paradoxical. Isn't it?

So that it was impossible to please the *milicos*, who'd taken great pains to transform Argentine society, especially the families of political prisoners, into a vast pool of curdled milk. No: the idea of uncurdling milk, or reversing the process of separating its elements while incorporating a couple of tons of snot of different textures and consistencies, was not going to work. All you can make with curds is some kind of cheese. And eliminating, so to speak, never adding any element that contributes to coagulation, or the coalition of the whey with . . . OK, that's enough.

But no. It was necessary to show the *milicos* that battles waged from a base made out of garbage, like theirs, would be lost. That *compañero*, who had been mine, who was mine, would continue to be so. And the effort of the *milicos* to keep us separated, by forcing me to leave the country while they moved him, meanwhile, from jail to jail, by freeing him just a month after my exile, by not permitting him to leave the country, had to be frustrated. With what people call, how frightful, with what people call love, with that thing nothing is known about, but that people have decided, as with most objects and elements, to give a name.

**85** And, in the meantime, there was Alberto. Who had a tangible affinity for Los Angeles and the beaches that the city seemed to be stuck to. And not with snot. Skinny, very skinny. Full of angles. Some of them critical. Argentine, from Mar de Plata, he shared with his brother and his brother's family, and so many other Argentines, Chileans, and Uruguayans, the perplexity of exile.

**86** I don't know the exact quantity, but let's say about fifteen. A mixture of fifteen little pieces of glass, different colors and very bright, some little rods, some, I don't know, things, tiny, enclosed between two walls at the end of a cardboard tube, or whatever, with enough freedom of movement and a little mirror placed I don't remember in what position, all those elements, arranged correctly, make a kaleidoscope. Also a hole through which it might be possible to observe the results of each fraction of revolution. Right? Because, if not, then what's it all for? A kaleidoscope: for infinite possibilities, for an inexhaustible variation of images, for an unexpected combination of tones, for a surprising succession of joys, of stirrings of the heart, of hallucinatory thrills that belie the difficult truth that nothing, ever, for anyone, will ever be the same again.

**87** Though with a whole lot of effort, perhaps we could manage to make it, in some way, similar. Because you have to stay on your feet.

**88** So, while my *compañero* walked the streets of Rosario, just liberated, trying to get rid of the headaches brought on by his attempts to understand life's multiplicities, I was fooling myself into believing it was possible to understand my own. I split my time between my job as a live-in maid and my friendship with Alberto. I returned to the sources: where linguistics were concerned, we studied Saussure. When it came to nocturnal activity we slept, on the weekends, more or less together. More or less, because the agreement was clearly defined: ours was a form of friendship that would change the minute the plane carrying my *compañero* descended into Los Angeles. And since those were the conditions and the agreement was firm, it was necessary that my *compañero* be informed of everything. And without subtlety: clearly, head on, extending him the same liberties. And the long telephone cable that spanned the American continent from end to end would facilitate my words, especially because his huge eyes would only be there in my imagination. Distance would soften the pain. It would distribute the rights to affection, to human contact, to the affirmation that one was, in spite of everything, alive, thoroughly alive.

Until the moment when we meet again. And from that instant, redoubling our vitality. Not depriving ourselves of the universal satisfaction of sticking our tongues out at the *milicos* across the length of America in all its immensity, in all the intensity of its madness. The two of us together, my *compañero* and I, embracing, two tongues sticking out, triumphant, satisfied, victorious.

It's okay to express the hurts, but the joys need to be expressed too. Whether because the joys are truths, or because they're lies, or illusions, or expressions of desire, or hallucinations, or because they're temper tantrums, or forms of disgust, or because they're only an intention or much more than that, or an imperious need, or because they're a practiced skill, the magisterial grace with which we prepare ourselves for.

**89** Slowly? Hmmm. I don't know. Not so much, I would say. Depending on the vehicle you choose, you might have the option of four or five speeds. Depending on what circumstance demands. Depending on the pace of their pursuit. Depending how you perceive, deep down in your muscles, the way in which the pieces of life are being torn from you, either quickly or slowly.

**90** Those regions where the origins are sustained, those in which beginnings are put forth and resolved, where the seeds are not permitted to make decisions, where one is never brave enough to allow oneself to lose, to abandon oneself to the sweet, dark seduction of failure, those areas, they are the ones that the sun allows to filter among the orifices that escape from the rain. And that is the task. The task of the hero. To find those spaces that, from their position of invisibility, shout, insult, offend because they can't be easily detected.

I remember the black girlfriend of that Chinese friend of mine, I remember the phonemes, the phrases of rejection. That she employed for the rejection. She worked doggedly to prevent anything from escaping any opening: not the sun, not the rain, not the wind, not the possible earthquakes. Nothing: complete and utter invasion. And why not, she said? And, to whom, to what, am I going to leave the orifices, the spaces? It seemed as though invasion was the condition that kept her alive. My Chinese friend observed. He didn't avoid the analyses that tempted him constantly. He watched her, quietly.

Always quiet. One day he moved his lips and described the alternatives to her, none. That he should marry her. That in her he had found the most shadowy, most distressing case possible. And that he felt himself chosen. A hero. That he was destined to find in her and in others the orifices through which she absorbed, sucked in, the powers of existence. That those powers should be shared more equitably between them, more . . . Aha, she said: aha. And accepted the proposal.

And there they are those two still, in the fight. In the thick of things, in the all-consuming mixing machine that is the intimate, universal battle. Out there, sort of swimming in the semi-liquid zones, in the regions where origins are sustained. Exiled from themselves. Exiled in each other. The foot of one on the other's hip. The rib of one in the future tumors of the other. Pieces of one brain in the blood stream of the other. The palm of one hand against the mouth and eyes of the other.


91 Because exile is something that can be measured by its length, by its width, by its depth, or by a combination of all of them, or by its utter emptiness. Or can it?


92 Those regions where the origins of strong desire are nurtured, the most visceral impulses, those are the ones I have decided to conquer. That's the only place I'll be satisfied building a home. My, shall we say, plot of land. A retreat provisioned with everything I need to resist until the last moment. Even against the last moment. Alone. Battling it. Pushing it to the limits of possibility. We go through life accumulating such dread of the end. A disgust for endings. Because as far as the death thing goes, no way.

Enough already. We've already died too much.

Like a pharaoh's burial chamber. With all the essentials.

What unimaginable, boundless delight there is knowing you are there, in one of that house's narrow rooms, its wooden floors half covered by thick, colorful carpets, your body weighing down a wicker rocking chair, a glimmer of light from a warm lamp, immortal, your left hand hanging over the arm of the chair and your right resting on your right thigh, absorbing energy, fingers a little tense, ready in the event you have to jot down a few of the mind's discoveries. Seated there, obeying the to and fro of the chair and of your brain, asking yourself questions and questions and more questions, digging into the reasons, interrogating the causes, investigating the foundations, sinking into the motives, swimming in the multicolored heap of motivations that keep human beings alive.

How did we manage to get here? So far away from ourselves. So close to our own guts? Do our surroundings consume us, or do they stabilize us, do the plodding innumerable spaces in between attack us?

**93** How did we end up by this sea? With air of this thickness, with the endless sounds of rock 'n' roll and blues running through every dimension of the mist? And this image, how is it that we land in front of this image that summons my shadow, my emotion and the anesthesia that alters the volume of my throat: the image of the man full of angles, we called some of them critical, seated before a sewing machine in the midst of a combination of blues and yellows in the grand kitchen in the grand mansion where I am a maid, doing his best to follow the outlines of a multicolored, stuffed frog that will end up full of millet, put up for sale in some crowded part of a city populated by transparencies?

Because there is no doubt that we prefer making little stuffed animals to working as servants. Maybe some day we'll transcend the aforementioned status.

How did I appear before this sea? Since when have I felt as though I'm sailing my own ship? Do I feel that I'm sailing my own ship? Am I sailing my own ship? Is there, has there been a ship? Have I arrived dissolved by the contradictory pressures of space? Disintegrated by the rarefied emptiness? Impelled by the horror of the immediacy of that final vertigo? Ruled by this state of amazement?

**94** Oh, yes, of course: they made sure I understood, without much subtlety, that transformations and mutations were possible. More than that: something to be celebrated. That their method was applicable to an infinite number of potential cases, including mine. That certain changes are necessary, and that one shouldn't be frightened by the prospect of transmuting a thought, a political position, by the idea of metamorphosis. In the end even Kafka changed his hero, his baby, into a cockroach, not to insult him but to demonstrate that cockroaches are as respectable as human beings. You could learn, by accepting such notions of flexibility, to get along with the other (enemy), understand him, justify him. You could even learn to enjoy the other, and to enjoy life with all its charms. It was possible, then, to remove all rigidity, all dogmatism from your mind. And not only that: you could be sure that what some erroneously call informing, is nothing more than a constructive manner of eliminating delinquency, of taking care of our own, of maintaining our mental and physical being at peak fitness, our presence in this world (which isn't eternal anyway, but put aside that near certainty of one's much-feared premature disappearance) and also our morale. Because you know you have to be constructive. Our future and our happiness depend on it. So I should have transformed myself into something other than what I am. Because it isn't always possible to be what you are. Aha, yes. Of course. What a strange idea that is. It isn't always possible to be what you are. Better to be, let's see, a piece of dough before it's baked. A daisy. An *imbunche*. A spoonful of sand. Half a bucket of cement (because a whole one's too much). They made sure I understood it without much subtlety. And with negligible power of conviction. But could they be so boorish as to try to compare the sea to incarceration? In the wards and in the cells of the mind water doesn't murmur and the backs of the waves don't gleam as they're mounted by the sun.

**95** And you'll have to keep on rethinking the grooves of the city with its new contents.

**96** You'll have to keep on rethinking the scenery because it's not true that it has limits. That's one of the old lies. There are no dimensions, there is no end to the length of the creaky, splintered boards. And infinity makes witnesses of us all. No one can avoid the limitless space.

With a leap, in just a few seconds we take in a lifetime, that or we go on slowly savoring the intensity of each movement, of each frivolity, we will observe, we will dance all the dances, or some of them, we will pretend to sleep and we will be betraying, or we will be asleep while others betray, we will construct or we will not manage to construct the most magnificent buildings we can imagine standing thousands of years from now, we will destroy the silence or the vestiges of old notions, we will be heroes or we will run and hide and cry, like heroes, and finally we will be witnesses. At every moment, and of everyone and of each one, and of ourselves.

**97** And so: aha, yes. The stuffed frog. The planet is stuffed with stuffed frogs. Filled with millet.

**98** And if you have the suppleness of spirit, the requisite audacity to relate the long neck of a giraffe to the long journey ahead of you, maybe a question will arise. If you could connect one giraffe's neck to another, using the necks of every giraffe in existence, and if all those necks together extended all along that road that awaits us, how far would it reach? Because it wouldn't be so bad to walk upon a giraffe's neck. Or many of them. They have those brown spots on their beige or yellow skin. Or blotches. To go, you know, leaping from one spot to another. Concentrating on the spots that look darker. From one dark spot to another. With a highlight here and there, but not enough to tempt you too much.

Because careful with the light. Watch out.

**99** Don't you? Don't you have to look out for luminosity?

Yes, be careful. And carefully go along seeking out the ambiguities between light and luminosity. Between lengths, distances, and stretched spots. Between lengths and lengths. Between stretched spots and stretched spots.

**100** Not worrying. Not disrupting the impulses (because if they're genuine impulses no one can disrupt them). Yes. Yes. Calm down. Washing the toilets. Scrubbing the bathtubs. Not barking. Instead, giving the dogs something to eat, the ones that are as big as horses and have all the patience of *nouveau riche* kids. And the self-control of a circus lion that's getting over the flu and hasn't eaten for weeks. Running the vacuum, not letting yourself get all bent out of shape each time that quadrangular machine knocks into the ineptitude of your ankles. Going up and down again between one floor and another with the vacuum cleaner over your shoulder as if you were an old burro. And not complaining. Accepting the fact that, at the very least, you're in good enough shape to argue with yourself about which is preferable: dragging an old burro or pushing a senile goat.

A surprising, disconcerting privilege: one that the dead don't enjoy.

**101** We will destroy silences and go along creating sounds that are, how shall we say, alternative. Some of them way too delicate, others voluminous, devastating. Practice, persistence, and time will tell if someone comes up with an original, moving lyric. In order to create a complete song.

**102** Meanwhile you have to get a car. To leave, get away on Friday afternoons, away from Pasadena to a friend's house, and then back on Sundays, also in the afternoon, to Pasadena. And for a few other maneuvers. And there is one, a car, that my boss' mother, already up in years, doesn't drive anymore. White. Which is terrible because the color of the car you drive is extremely important. White: an historical burden. Toyota Corolla. True, very well maintained. How embarrassing. White and well cared for. How unbelievably disgusting. And the skinny, angular guy so gratified by the spectacle of someone whose favorite color is black driving a white car. And giving directions. Good ones, of course. Because in so many years of exile there have only been two accidents, and none caused by yours truly, the friend of the angular fellow. Two tickets, both for speeding, that the driver of this immaculate Toyota is proud of.

**103** So let's not slow down. Not here nor there. Not in this or in anything.

**104** And if each one of those little pieces of colored glass were a word, and if each one of those tiny little things were a comma, a period, how delightful to go along executing tiny turns of two or three degrees, and then suddenly a turn of ninety degrees. To go along seeing what? To go along trying. Measuring. Giving the blood's rhythm an opportunity to accelerate. To dance. To stop in a heartbeat. To enjoy the combinations. The contrasts. The lack of attachment, the joyful freedom of throwing a tiny piece of glass into the trash and from the same can picking out a shinier one, and making it your own, that you can discover smiling widely from within the text.

**105** Indifference, ingratitude for adolescent loves, the literary, that sometimes needs experiences like exile to recover space in its own insides.

**106** The new light, that never walks alone but rather makes her own shadow accompany her, contains other shadows as well. But its own, the one that never abandons it, what it really does is act like a bodyguard. Because the new light is eternally confused. It suffers from fears. It needs to be cared for, protected, defended. It needs the contrasts provided by its shadow and others, those that dance inside it, with the whiteness that its own presence emits, to understand itself. In order to understand why those who are falling, in ones, threes or big groups, landing in its sphere of influence, look around, observe, bite their lips, press their lips together, wrinkle their brow, squint their eyes to focus their gaze on the distance with greater precision, debate, argue, speculate, smile, move their arms, their legs, a little nervous, maybe looking for peace, greet each other, say good-bye, hug each other, look each other in the eye, from the corner of their eyes, restrain each other, pursue each other, understand each other, fix their gaze on a random point in space, try to breathe deeply, sometimes manage to, sometimes not quite, but don't stop trying; they eat very little sometimes, at times they gorge themselves endlessly, they try out diets to slim down, or to gain a little weight, since they've been run down. They go running in the parks; well, that and even more, but always as if everything were random, as if everything mattered very little, as if the only real priority were something that isn't there.

**107** The light that spreads itself over the vain happinesses, upon the blind tranquilities, upon the rivers, the skies and the mountain chains that form the backdrop for the grand drama that the Northern Hemisphere has put on since the beginnings of its history. That's the light I'm talking about.

**108** The light that for a short time will shine more brightly, strengthened by constantly exerting itself against the resistance.

**109** Because you will have to resist. You will have to oppose the new light. You can't privilege it with the power of bestowing forms. At least we can't, we who've come to these regions by the unreal, uncertain fortune of not being assassinated in other latitudes. In our own. Those that we at any rate don't possess. And that don't possess us either.

In spite of the dependencies. Of the umbilical cords. Of the loves, the old ones and the more or less recent ones. Of what some of us call political conscience and what imbeciles call guilt. Of what the ignorant call traumas and what those of us who know what's what call the process of recovering strength. In spite of the rain, of the familiar agglomeration of trash in the streets, of the damp cold and of those summers on the Rosarian beaches of La Florida or La Arenera, or on the Costanera of Buenos Aires. Of the gatherings in downtown cafés. Of love put into practice for the first time. The second time. The third time.

And I prefer to stop my list here. Because I need to walk. Not drag myself along: to walk. So let us now return to new latitudes. The ones we don't possess. The ones that don't possess us either.

**110** How are you supposed to keep your guard up if there is no active, potential enemy? How are you supposed to exercise, strengthen your muscles if you're not going to use them eventually?

**111** Eventually.

**112** It was here, it had already been here for a while, flowering and fluttering, the Committee for Democracy in Argentina (CDA), for anyone who needed to identify it from the outside or the inside. Or from any other angle. There it was, with its points of pride, tasks to be performed, inevitable squabblings of fighting cocks, and battles to pay the rent on its little downtown space. There it was. Political workspace. In spite of the surprising length of the discussions designed to distill at least twenty competing opinions about the Falkland Islands War into a single yes or no vote. That would of course come later. But not because anyone would dare to make a decision, other than the one our momentarily heroic Argentine president had made. Heroic and sober. On the table was no less important an issue than the wording of the manifesto that was about to be published in the Los Angeles *La Opinión*: either an endorsement of the defense of invaluable and strategic lands, or a campaign to preserve the lives of several generations of Argentine and British youth. Tough decision! Yet so many arduous, extended deliberations would be required to (what do I know?) to arrive at something that, in any case, no one could agree upon.

**113** Simple and painful: that describes, in a nutshell, the end of various things: my relationship with the *compañero* with the blond-gray curls, who had once been in an Argentine prison cell and who had landed on the beaches of Los Angeles one year ago, who had stuck to one side of the manifesto, that wasn't the same as mine; my relationship

with the CDA; my relationship with some of its members.
Especially with Raúl and Marisa. The same ones who had
approved that brown, empty miniskirt waiting to be filled
with a round butt, sufficiently firm, like mine.

**114** To stay there, half-seated, half-lying
down, with your listless arms, empty,
hanging over the edges, the borders,
your legs along the length of the bed, sofa, your feet upon
one of the great big pillows, two great big pillows, legs half
open, shaven, unshaven, doesn't matter. No skirt, no
pants. No sweater, no t-shirt. No bra, no panties. Your
eyes gazing absently at some point in motion, or at rest, of
the future, of your own or someone else's. Or both. One
or two curls, ringlets, spilling over your forehead, your
shoulders, lending a bit of brightness to the air, reddish,
or yellowish, a little golden, or blue, depending on which
pane the midday sun has decided to pass through, if in
fact the window has some colored glass in it somewhere.
And if it's midday. With some kind of stuff on your skin,
that's not disagreeable to the touch, only a bit, let's say,
sticky, but not exaggeratedly so, because you might have
just taken a shower a little while before. And you've been,
for some time, spreading the almond and cocoa cream
over all, or almost all, the surface of your body. Or the
other, the one with wheat and avocado. Or the one with
the incredible mix of fruits that doesn't include bananas
thank God, because God only knows what else you might
do with it. Whatever occurs to you. A smoothie, for example. You think? Or Johnson's Baby Oil. Or maybe you
haven't been spreading anything at all. And your skin is
dry to the touch. Or that stuff, a little bit of sweat, salty
sweat, sweet, soft, deeply your own. Or your neighbor's.
Your neighbor's sweat. Because that's also a possibility.

To stay there: Doot. Da-doo . . . Just like that.

Without any music. None. No currents of air in motion. Not even the ones caused by the in and out of breathing. Or maybe with a certain music, the kind that comes in through narrow passageways, the narrow distance between the window frame and that metal strip on the edge of the glass, the window without the colored glass, not frosted or opaque or engraved, nothing special. That window. A certain musicality laid over the perception of a possible panorama, words, that will compose part of what some of us who have decided to look ourselves in the eye, faced squarely forward, would call the future. Do you understand? Because the future can't be found in anyone's eyes. The future, that thing that is not findable yet desperately sought after, stalked, that which incites anxieties, questions, tickling sensations and prolonged silences, that thing, gurgles in your intestines. Not in your eyes. In the interstices, in the tangle of tissues in the inner walls of your intestines. There, there it is generated, there it is debated, heat enters, boils, intercepts opposing forces, grows, burns obstacles, surges, mobilizes, dances, shows itself, hides, withdraws, spills out, lets itself be seen, disappears. There is no future in anyone's eyes. All the possibilities are collected in the most ingenious laboratory in existence. There where the exit route begins for all that is considered disposable.

To stay that way. Quiet. No complications.

But no. It's impossible. You have to go out and work. Earn a living. You have to go out the door and remember everything: that these aren't the main streets of your own city, that the only sky you can see belongs to a foreign hemisphere; that neither here, nor there, nor on the border of some other abyss has the light decided to make itself public, to officially declare itself a curve and to follow me around the corner when I turn; that it's not raining today; that the clouds are heavy, wide, and deform in the wind.

# 115

On one side, there's the world map. Carefully placed, hanging on the left wall of the room that, in 1997, belongs to my daughter. My daughter who is already thirteen years old. And on the other side, affixed against the whiteness of the right wall facing the window, a giant red and black poster of the diaphanous, warrior beauty of Che.

I'd taken a brief lie down on my daughter's bed to rest from the immensity. I was trying to narrow the limits of what surrounded me. I was trying to adjust them to the dimensions of my body. To gather myself together so I could regain my own form. Such an expansive wave that creaks, that originates in, that comes rumbling out from some internal impulse. So much spilling over of yourself. So I made myself comfortable without much ado along the length of the bed and placed a few pillows around me, imagining that they were a coffin. And after a while I fell more or less asleep. When I opened my eyes I looked around and the first thought I had was Aha, here I am. Here I am awake again, between Che Guevara and the destiny of the world. Between the planisphere and the destiny of man. And my breathing was shallow, I asked myself if it wouldn't be better to just adapt, recognize that there are no measures or limits, that the spilling over of yourself is the only condition, that permits us to stay alive. I couldn't breathe deeply without throwing to the floor, with some violence, the pillows that were trying to change me into an only myself.

It's a prodigious daily task accepting the immensity, understanding that your self is just the workings of your mind, that each molecule that composes you is another, a different one, and that each one is everyone else, and the body we think is our own is so scattered, so dispersed, that each one of us is a jolly spilling over of molecules, and that we're disseminated in life, in the entire length and the entire width and the entire depth of each and every permutation of the air that, nevertheless and with difficulty, let's say, contains us.

**116** Because we dedicate ourselves with such pleasure to making existing differences thrive. And for those that don't exist, we invent them.

**117** And no one says that it's not appropriate. Or apt, that game. Or just. There's a lot happening on the road between accepting immensity and creating differences. There's an awful lot happening.

**118** The year was ending, in Pasadena. 1981. Twelve splendid months in the Pasadena house were ending with a book of poems almost complete and a novel coming along. And the *compañero* with the gray-blond curls was arriving. He was disembarking from the Aerolíneas Argentinas airplane that was depositing him in the Los Angeles airport. That was placing him at the beginning of a practicable path: that of accepting the vastness. That of visualizing, along its whole width, the dance of our floating molecules. The great desolation that keeps us occupied and agile. But in order to accept you first have to understand.

**119** The wild side: that of understanding. That of multiple penetrations. That of grasping the real and true profundity of our own openings.

**120** Wild.


**121** But saying wild is like not saying anything. It's like saying I'm sorry. It's like
laughing at yourself. Like laughing at
anyone who's ignorant of the reasons for our laughter.
Sterile. So it's better to save yourself the epithets.

Seated among the noisy and abundant audience in a
theater (and especially if our seat happens to be perfectly
situated in a corner against the wall in the last or second-
to-last row) it is possible to recognize faces and shadows,
the shadows in the faces, the faces in the shadows. When
that interplay of light and darkness, of flashes and
eclipses also envelops the open spaces of the stage, it is
easier to interpret the dilemmas that are being posited,
between pauses in the singing and the rhythms, the features of the musicians we love and who offer up their
sweat, their vibrations and the assorted fluids from their
throats to us.

The long, wide and dark moustache of one of them,
one of the four, that splays out, adhering to the strong,
dependable face that displays it, of the nose and mouth
that try and hide it, which enters and leaves his vocal reg-
ister as if it were the very words that are, that are being,
sung. As if it were a graphic representation, darkly graphic, of its own meaning. It leaps and disappears and returns
to its place completing the assigned task, satisfied in the
knowledge of a job well done. Pancho's moustache.
Romerito's. And the power, the authority of the voice
that's enveloping us even to the farthest reaches of History.

That one. History. The one who usually pretends not
to notice. Who passes right by without noticing the quick
steps of the events as they glide along on skates.

Enveloping us. Tightening our chest, that cavity where our vital organs are firmly planted. The structural hollow where all our worrieds, our emotionals, our sensitives, our exposeds, our outstandings, our inspireds, our builders, our makers go to live. Our creators. Our parents. And ourselves, the parents of our parents. The cavity where our dead go to live.

The voice that protects us and spreads us out. That opens us, unraveling the winding paths, leaving the passageways clear for any kind of bubblings, gushings, fatal paroxysms.

Because sometimes behind the stage curtains harsh whispers are gathering, creating sharp forms in the velvet. That make you think of hidden metal barrels pointed at the musicians' backs, reminding them of the things that they should, of the things that they can and of the things that they shouldn't. But why? Why is it that we make associations like this so easily?

Death shouldn't be an option. You have to keep singing. You have to keep pronouncing all the words. You have to emit the highest-pitched sound, you have to modulate to the last syllable to surpass the limit, to erase it with shouting, to turn it to mist, to transcend it.

Here, there or farther away. Where is only a word, not a worry. The obstructions, the impediments to the exercise of our internationalism that we must comply with. Nope. They're not allowed.

And so, without too much complaint or much blubbering, after having avoided it for years, after trying to elude so many pointy forms in the velvet of successive stages, of the large, of the narrow, of the full of schizophrenia, it was necessary to retreat. That wasn't the worst of the fatalities though there was no way to get rid of the sadness, it wasn't more chilling than the threats but there was no way to escape the rage, it represented the end of the persecutions, but it led you to confront a new form of History where you already had your own, and didn't need any originality or any new invention or any surprising new piece of news. Those particular moments in life when, and there are oh so many of them, so many, we hope, please, we beg, we pray, that no one brings us any news of any kind or category.

Good-bye Cosquín. Good-bye Rosario. Good-bye Córdoba.

As for my tail, the Devil may care for it. And the color of my feathers, let the chattering parrot watch over it. As for my own relief, I'll leave that to my conscience.

And we'll go along, more or less walking, more or less leaping, more or less dragging our feet. Trying to synchronize the movements of both our legs, to coordinate the rhythms. So that one doesn't try to move ahead while the other one gets in the way. Right? They get tangled up.

And so on and so on.

Until a landing takes place in the mist, manifestations of admiration and affection upon unknown faces in charge of receiving the new South American political exile, unknown noses and eyes representing Amnesty International, the International Red Cross, and as much internationality and human rights and kindnesses that fit into the spaces between the country that creates the horror and propagates it, and their own made-up pathos, the kind that comes from supposedly trying to save humanity from any conceivable injustice. And also, a few acquaintances, maybe. For example, the exile who arrived, under similar circumstances, a few months before. And maybe also, as in the case of Pancho's moustache, the woman who waited on him forever.

Let's see what we can do around here. Maybe start a new musical group. With my voice and my compulsions. With my interpretive talents and urgent artistic needs. With the support of my wife, brand new *compañera*, and the recognition of a public that, if it isn't familiar with me, is at least willing to get to know me. Singing at private parties given by well-meaning, nostalgic Argentines, at shows organized by Argentines, Chileans, Nicaraguans, groups of people and families that surely bought my records in their own countries when they could still run the risk of taking a step forward on the battlefield. They're here for reasons not unlike my own and will understand my voice, my tenor shouts and my silences. They'll be my audience in Los Angeles. And in the rest of the United States. Yes. They'll be the system of catapults that, between one performance and another, will propel my poetic and political word, folkloric and southern, saddened but firm and convincing.

But during the time it takes to reach that place, you've got to eat. Eating may imply work. But work shouldn't imply having to communicate with anyone in English. That'd take too many years. It could last an eternity. So work in Spanish. I've heard about what's possible plenty of times, about what's reasonable to expect. The newcomers paint walls. They clean offices. They scour houses. They scrub mansions. With enough luck they can even manage to attain the exalted status of babysitter.

C'mon, Pancho, let's go, with that powerful moustache of yours, that fair weather look in your dark eyes, which are as full of sounds as your throat, those imminent entrances that fill up your face nearly to the sides of your generous head. Let's go. Like everything else in life, this is fleeting. While it lasts we'll meet new people, friends, other singers, and musicians who are looking for a leader with the necessary magnetism. Indispensable to create a folk group that not only sings but speaks.

As you're making your way, there's this man, also Argentine, who was an architect in Buenos Aires, and who after some years managed to pass the exam and get his builder's license, and even though you aren't a builder or a carpenter and haven't ever done that kind of work, you can, I don't know, give it a try, maybe work for him. We've already spoken and he's willing to give you a job, you'll learn something new, you'll help him paint walls, clean up the mess that's left after each job, and he says he'll take you along to buy the materials he needs for each house he fixes, because what he usually does is repairs, so that you begin to learn what everything is and what it's used for, because as I told you construction is very different here than back in Buenos Aires or Rosario, here they don't use brick, nothing heavy or hard, they use wood or particle board, because this is a seismic zone. He also says that he'll tell you the names of the tools and materials in English, and that way you'll have to learn the language. Not that you wouldn't be able to survive in Spanish in Los Angeles, especially if you're going to be working in construction, but you've got no idea of the enormous freedom and independence that being able to express yourself in English will give you.

And a car. That's another thing you have to think about. Here, in Los Angeles, you can't make it without a car. With this job you can begin to save a few bucks, and you can buy a used car, that doesn't have too many problems, the most important thing is that you don't get stuck in the middle of the freeway. Japanese cars are the best, a Toyota, for example, that doesn't use much gasoline. And that way you'll get ahead little by little. You'll see. Yes, you'll see. There's everything here. You'll be able to survive, and at least here no one will be giving you orders about what to sing and what not to sing. You'll have to build up a following, but that happens naturally. That's part of an exile's life. You'll do it, remember. You already have a secure and developed artistic life. At least in Argentina. You know perfectly well what you have to do to continue it, even in another part of the world. You don't have to pass any tests like Celia, the pediatrician friend of José Laborde, who didn't make it, who never passed her exams in English. Now she's stuck making little baskets with dried flowers. And worse, trying to sell them.

But hey, that's life's ups and downs for us. At least we can say we're alive. You and I might not be in any position to paint any wall right now.

Romerito. The immortal. The best voice on Earth, along with Negra Sosa. The legend of Rosario. Now in Los Angeles. Little by little. You'll see. Life is long. Not for everyone, I know, I know.

It's like a merry-go-round. You know? You get yourself situated, more or less, I don't know, find a little spot, like a wooden horse, not the one from Troy, a less pretentious one, and you start going in circles. When the guy running the thing pushes the button, of course. Not before or after. Facing forward, because a merry-go-round horse can't look from side to side. Right? Rigidly maybe, yes, why should I deny it, a little bit stiff because of the circumstances, because you have to keep fighting, but looking ahead, suddenly something, a little something, almost indiscernible, indicates there's been a change. And the change is that something's begun to move. And the merry-go-round is spinning. Going around in circles. It takes off. And it's simple: if you have the audacity, the vitality, you make the leap and escape the circular motion. You leave the merry-go-round with one less horse, but you're the owner of your own gait. More or less, of course. Because nothing is absolute. There are few cases like this, but every once in a while someone comes along who makes it and surprises us all. And those are the ones who vindicate us. The ones who save the rest of us. The ones who make us proud to be who we are. You, Pancho, you can't let us down. The Argentine exile in Los

Angeles depends on your voice.

Wild, ladies and gentlemen. Wild.

**122** The mist, that unfurls its gray majesty upon the habitable skies.

**123** And the other option, the one that becomes obvious when the clouds take on all the colors, all the brilliance.

**124** And the subject of our desire. And the object of our necessity. And the reasons for our anxieties. The ones we will always return to.

**125** Wide, expansive, green, the green garden behind the house owned by those progressive Californians, tall and blonde, endowed with two sets of blue eyes (a pair for each of them), average height with mild expressions like goose down pillows. She of slow and knowing steps, he with unruly hair and fuzz on his long legs, more or less masculinely crossed. More than a garden, a park. A forest. Several years living together, married. No children. Lots of reading, lots of keeping current on adversities in the poor countries of the world, especially Central and South America. And the slight, strained smile of knowing, really knowing, what good members of Amnesty International you are. A wide, deep forest, tennis court. Swimming pool. Her shorts white, barely distinguishable from her legs. So much whiteness here and there. And that gigantic map on the living room wall, riddled with little red magnetic flags that celebrate their having experienced, really experienced, all those places, delightful little towns, in poor countries, like Machu Picchu, Tierra del Fuego, Cancún.

You sit down on a white plastic armchair, with soft, springy cushions in white and green stripes, still a little bit damp from the incursion of the seaside morning, from its dew, from the dimensions of its turbulence. You sit down, thinking: my pants don't matter. So they'll get wet. So the dampness will seep in and get caught in the seams. At any rate they'll dry out. They'll manage. Because I'm not going to play the delicate flower now, I'm not going to let them think I'm a crybaby who comes undone over the littlest things. No, no. The fact is you're here because you've been oh so thoughtfully invited to spend a sunny day, a day decorated by multicolored salads, soon to be inundated with the smell of barbecue, enough for forty people, all of whom are very interested in "hearing the details of your experience in jail, the political situation in Argentina, the reality of the concentration camps, the role of the Church in the repression, because words like that straight from the mouth of someone who's been through what you've been through are an incomparable motivation for the new members of Amnesty." You haven't come here to dance, to play the model. So there.

So fast, that one. With a rag in one hand, and a gesture that says, don't sit down, let me dry it for you, and those sweet wafting vapors, like mango nectar, that you perceive at the level of your chest, your breasts, your stomach. Thanks, Janis. Because you've lived through so much pain. Because you've gone without so much, save that which you've provided for yourself through sheer force of will.

And so you sit down on the soft, springy, dry cushion, you sit down, you lean your ascetic ass gently, then heavily, so pure it's almost Mormon, and you start to pick up on the eagerness and the empathy and the tolerance and the condescension of forty faces that hover, that suction, that make eye contact, that avoid eye contact, that wander, that think they understand, that ignore and that feel themselves to be, without a doubt, indispensable, irreplaceable, illustrious. And so it is that, from your own intestines, all the terrors, all the phobias, all the character flaws, all the questions and the urgent need for answers, attack. The questions: where? Where? Where am I? What the hell am I doing here? What planet are these human-like creatures from? What do they really want or need? What can I really give them? Which is more genuine: my conviction that my testimony raises the consciousness of these headstrong people or the joy that spills forth from my insides when an eloquent, subservient hand dries the seat I'm about to rest my behind on for the rest of the day?

And the urgent need for answers. Right at that moment, when the only thing required of me is a tale, emotionally delivered of course, of the death, of the life that I've emerged from. Right now, it so happens that a demand for answers appears. With that tone. With that pressing little tone.

**126** Overlooked, outrageous, inappropriate, the objects of our desire, of our necessity, of our anguish.

**127** What you've just told us is incredible. Completely overwhelming.
So then, now, what's your legal, immigration status (all this in English, or with translators as intermediaries). I entered the country as a tourist. Oh,

you're not a refugee then. Well, no, I came here as a tourist. Yes, she came as a tourist but now she's seeking political asylum. Where did you request it? Here, in Los Angeles. But they didn't give it to you in Argentina before you left? No, they didn't give it to me. No, they didn't give it to her. That's why she had to come as a tourist. Didn't you go to the U.S. Consulate in Buenos Aires? Yes, I went twice. They said no. That they wouldn't give me asylum or refugee status because of my previous record. What do you mean they didn't give it to you because of your previous record. That's ridiculous. Without your previous record what need would you have to seek asylum? Yes, it's a contradiction, I know, but that's how it went. But, you know, this isn't France. It isn't Sweden. They told me that they didn't want people from the left, subversives, here. I didn't get a refugee visa. So then, what did you do? I applied for a tourist visa through the travel agency that sold me the ticket. Like any other person that wants to go on a trip. And since that travel agency had worked with the U.S. Consulate for years, they automatically stamp the pile of passports that go to the consulate every day. No questions. No nothing. So I managed to leave Argentina and come here to Los Angeles.

There now. There now, my dear. Everything is OK. You're surrounded by friends here, people who are going to give you what you need, and in the end you're going to get your asylum, and little by little things will fall into place. And your friend will get out of the country, and the two of you will be reunited here, and if they don't give him asylum, he'll enter as a tourist too. He'll follow the same procedure. You'll both be OK. You'll find a place where no one comes after you, or threatens you, or tortures you or wants to kill you. We'll take care of your well-being. Whatever you two need.

So what are you doing about getting asylum? Working with Al Furman. He's a lawyer, a member of

Amnesty. Oh, yes, yes. I know him. He's a great guy. He's getting papers for a bunch of ex-political prisoners from Latin America. He has a lot of experience. He knows what he's doing and has a real sense of justice. He's exactly what you need. Everything will be all right, you'll see.

Are you hungry? Thanks so much for your story, you know? Thanks so much for reliving that horror and letting us participate in what your people are going through. We need to hear all this testimony. It's an enormous help when you speak to us that way, so directly. The new people need to understand, and you've really helped with that today. Thanks. Thanks so very much.

You must be hungry. The barbecue is almost ready. Look at that table full of salads. Look at the colors. How fresh. So many different shapes and sizes. Don't think we don't feel guilty. But at least you're here with us, so now we can share what we have. Aren't the colors just incredible? And the sky? Isn't the light just gorgeous? It's afternoon already. You've been in Los Angeles for two months. And now summer is coming to an end. Theoretically. You'll notice that in Los Angeles it's summer almost all year long. And you feel an arm around your shoulders. And you see a woman's smiling face coming towards you, determined. And a young couple, the girl pregnant, attempts with the best of intentions to give you a group hug and in unison cry out something like, God, you look so young and strong . . . Thank you, so so much, for being with us today. And the joyous slowness of an old brown-haired man, compact and kind who tells me he fought in the Spanish Civil War. (If you want to write meee, yooou will know right where to find me, if you want to write meee, yooou will know right where to find me: On the front line of the battle, standing in the line of fire. Aaahn the front line of the baaattllle, staaandiing in the line of fiiiiere) who also hugs me, who takes my two hands in his own, warm and energetic.

And I hear the chirp of my own voice, multitudinous, reverberating in my joints, my knees, the vertebrae of my spine, shouting, please, please, I want so much, I want so much to live. I'm dying, every day I'm dying to live.

And your own urgent list of questions keeps growing: How? How? With what peace? With what calm, with what tranquility is it possible to breathe in such a way that air gets in? So that the oxygen does its work of purifying the blood that keeps us in motion. That gives us movement, that sets our rhythm. Our proportions. With what peace?

**128** A vegetable soup in which the delicate pieces of carrot float where they will. No, no, no, no, no. Who said that's what I want to eat?

**129** Disconnect. Disengage. Dispossess. Discombobulate. Disown. Disarm. Disarticulate. Disentangle. Disturb. Dismantle. Disperse. Dissociate. Displace. Disrupt. Dissever. Dismount. Disable. Dislodge. Disunite. Dispel. Disjoint. Disquiet. Disorder. Dishevel. Dissect. Disemploy. Disfigure. Disassemble. Dissolve. Disembody. Disintegrate. Disuse. Displume. Disband. Disrespect. Dismember. Disenfranchise. Dislink. Discharge. Discase. Dislocate. Disbrain. Dispose. Disempower. Disappoint. Disorient. Dissipate. Disaggregate. Discern.

**130** Disrobe.

**131** The disrobed vision of your figure, illuminated by moonbeams in this moment of the night, in this place of the night, does not move me. The nakedness of your insides, the sight of your inflamed liver, of your intestines, the possibility that the open nakedness of your body gives me, your bodies, to count the palpitations of your organs so interconnected and at the same time so blissfully independent, doesn't affect me. I keep letting my gaze wander around the margins of my own body with a kind of distracted tone, almost real, almost, and the perspective of what seems to be a genuine emptiness, an immense nothing surrounding me, doesn't frighten me. It is the representation of liberty. It is the open space where I will go on placing the creations, the inventions born of my free state.

**132** How is it that we got to the shores of this sea?

You could smell it. Upon the faces of the country's inhabitants, violet, geometric shadows were being projected, produced by the enormous grenade on its way to imminent impact. It was possible to perceive the metallic odor that guided our heads toward that expected, concrete sky of everyday life. And there it was. Coming closer. There was no mystery as to its origins. No doubts about its nucleus, comprised of a singular explosive and its fragmentable shell. So the intermittent joys started to disappear from our muscles, and the accumulated adrenaline began to instill tension and incredulity. The fears and the forms that defiance would take. You could see it and you could observe it with its desire to diminish the distance. Green. Grayish and green. With a detonator willing to do anything. The impact caught us all together, planning the details of our resistance. And the explosion altered both our numbers and our power of decision. Suddenly we were splinters, or the aftermath of a giant explosion, splinters of ourselves, splinters of a whole. And you could see us crossing the sky in arching movements, elliptical, rapid, impelled toward geographic multiplicity, toward an infinity of destinations, without any chance to say good-bye to the ones who were lost to sight in the explosion.

**133** I no longer say that I'm not leaving you because our separation would be another victory for the *milicos*. I no longer even think it. It doesn't rush from the orifices of my brain. Now, given the circumstances, the veritable triumph of the *milicos* over our political, social, personal and private lives would be that I make the heroic decision to stay by your side listening attentively, or not so attentively, to the creakings of your voice as it passes through your throat, that usually stays shut, to let out Oh, yes, these streets, these streets of Los Angeles, are narrower than those of Buenos Aires. Oh, yes, these parks are so common and everyday, and on top of that boring, there're no people, but the ones in Rosario, on the other hand, they overflow with life, with children running, shouting, playing. Here people hate each other, if something happens to you on the street, if you have some sort of accident or you get sick, everyone walks right over you, no one comes to your aid, no one helps you. North Americans are so cold and selfish, they walk around spreading their spotless, hypocritical smiles right and left, without feeling any of it. We, the Argentines, in Argentina, we couldn't have more problems, but at least we know what solidarity is. Here no one has the slightest idea what the word means. And don't even talk to me about English. I'm not going to bother learning it. Its far too limited as a language to embrace the boundless expressiveness of the Argentines. English words aren't sufficient to perfectly, precisely represent my ideas, to enunciate, formulate all my questions, to display the complexity of my answers.

What's happened. Tell me. There aren't any fears that you don't have embedded in your muscles. No insecurities that you've forgotten to acquire. No phobias that you've opted not to develop. And I need an enormous empty space around me. Something along the lines of a wide, white, transparent disk that contains me, that preserves me, that emancipates me. That offers me the indispensable oxygen, *compañero*.

**134** And so enough.

**135** E-nough.

**136** I was looking for an equation. I looked into all the possible combinations: intelligence with indifference to life's pleasures. Intelligence with physical ugliness. Intelligence with physical beauty. Intelligence with good physical health. Intelligence with every kind of physical handicap. Intelligence with an insatiable desire for food and sex. Intelligence with all manner of vices and weaknesses. Intelligence with mental illnesses. The crutches upon which it is possible to support oneself in order to keep in motion. Guinea pig: Samuel Johnson. I read him, I dissected him, I scrutinized him, I held him tight, I held him at a distance, I brought him close again, I poked my fingers in his guts, I moved them in all directions, I observed the reactions, I let him rest, I woke him up again, I asked him hundreds of questions, I didn't give him the opportunity to answer them. I asked him to go, to leave me in peace. If, when looking at Samuel Johnson's digestive apparatus none of his organs made me hungry, neither the salvageable ones nor the disposable ones, then it's better to take a nap. Maybe I was in desperate need of another Samuel. Beckett? Molloy.

**137** Because all these combinations are comparable to a seemingly calm stroll along the beach. Along one of the beaches. It's possible to fancy oneself one or more of those combinations. Especially when sinking your feet in the damp sand means to elucidate. To circumscribe anguish, to delineate the reasons for anguish from the reasons for happiness. What opens us to weeping versus what opens us to a moment of satisfaction? So complicated.

To understand why the brush of an elbow on a sheet that smells of laundry detergent sends a sensation of opening, of surrender, through all my pores, a daring desire to roar with laughter, and the next minute make me burst into one of those long laments, monotonous, automatic, full of hiccups and other respiratory difficulties, during which you discover that you are really crying for others. That other people's sorrows are, also, your own, or that they're not, is another of the things we have to elucidate. If it mattered.

**138** And when my elbow on that sheet unleashes that laughter, I'm laughing like crazy with my *compañeras* during a recess in the courtyard of Villa Devoto prison, about some nonsense, some joke, the sudden flowering of a good mood, the cleverness of one of us. And when my elbow on that sheet unleashes that cry, I'm crying with rage at the impossibility of restraining the hand of a torturer as it moves towards a *compañero's* testicles, electric cattle prod in hand.

Strategies of the brain, that remind us, second by second, that we haven't abandoned the land of our birth in order to indulge in some frivolous little vacation, however emotionally satisfying it may be.

**139** Shadows, right? Those forms that get diffused into different shades of gray, encrusted, diamonds mounted, on the surface of the moon, imperturbable for an infinity of time. And the sadness of not having lived enough to have had the opportunity to dream, standing upon the lunar surface, about the perfection of the forms, of the shadows, of the luminosities, of the contents of the Earth.

**140** But then each time you come back to life. You're resuscitated, if you can believe it. You employ all your faculties, all your tricks. You let your ingenuity have free reign and open up like a peacock's tail, showing off all its colors and designs. And then there's boasting. Of course. Because what's the point of having so much wisdom, of having gotten so far, if you can't have the opportunity to serve, if only, as an example. A little example.

Faced with each fright, faced with each sudden shock, faced with each indignation, faced with each sensation of drowning, the thing to do is find the instant where you can fix your pupils on some point of the long line that separates the blue of the sky from the blue of the water. That unites them. And you grow. All of a sudden you grow, you expand, you manage to invade the surfaces, the depths, the heights.

## 141    Other people's sorrows.

## 142
The green of the skies, the purple of the grass extended to the limits that the eyes can reach, the almost golden, somewhere between the golden and black reflection of the shadow of the birds in their circular flight above the heads of living cows, white, white and meditative. The orange of the toads' eyes. The blue thickness of their nails. The estrangement. What others would call nostalgia. The effort to understand the whys. The slowness of the looks that we wish were more energetic, more electric. The interconnection of each previous step, of each new link hooking onto the chain of apparent impossibilities. The lack of transparency in the rain, when it rains. And also when it doesn't rain. The tangential nature of everyday occurrences. The forms that oxygen acquires when it penetrates the bronchial tubes and fills, halfway, perhaps both lungs. The way in which it adapts to new respiratory circumstances. The ease with which we see what we want to see, we don't see what we want to see, we see what we don't want to see, we don't see what we don't want to see. And the green of the skies.

## 143
I need a cup of coffee, strong and sweet, instant and stirred, stirred, stirred. Stirred until the cup's nearly broken. But no. I'm not going to break it. I'm going to do everything I can to avoid that awkward moment when my compulsions leave me without my favorite of my more than

twenty cups. The plain black one. And since you have to recognize that obsessions rule the lives of some of us, I have to admit that mine could potentially leave me with no coffee at all. Because I'm certainly not going to drink it out of any other cup. It's the black one or none. So it's fine then to stir as long as I stop before I'm faced with the ultimate consequences.

**144** I need a strong cup of coffee. Today is the day of the coming of e-nough. Of removing from the apartment on Stanley and Santa Monica Blvd. my books, my novel about prison, just finished and title-less (and just read, in part, by that Chilean writer who they introduced me to, and oh, shit, is exiled in Mexico, not in Los Angeles), my panties, my jeans, my pictures. My other manuscripts. My old feelings of love for he who was my *compañero*. Because that has to be moved too with all your belongings. With your body. Clutched between your legs and which, together with your mind, will be happy, in the future, about having saved the remnants, those things that are indispensable for the day when we decide to reinvent that which some people put under the category of past.

**145** And adding a few kangaroos and spiders to it. And trimming away the weeds and dry branches. And attaching some alternative colors. And outlining it, scribbling on the dividing lines you drew so confidently with the pencil of that knowledge, the wisdom of back then.

**146** And also e-nough of this job that sounds better than scrubbing toilets with one hand and writing poems with the other, than selling insulation (without asbestos, which is of course carcinogenic) for the roof and the walls, so that energy doesn't escape, that's ordinarily quite hard to find, so that our little bit of heat doesn't fly away, that little bit of heat, please, don't let our little bit of heat escape. Enough of this job where the owner, caught up in the rapture of artistic inspiration, creates floral arrangements with dried or wooden flowers, or strange synthetic materials, while I, over huge tanks of pure, the purest, bleach submerge the blooms whose original colors the artist doesn't like. Breathing (me, not the artist) the acidic and corrosive vapors of my own stupidity. Because I have to find another job. I've had enough of this one.

**147** And besides I want to go to Mexico and live with that Chilean writer.

**148** And we think, we whisper: . . . Doot da-doo da-doo . . .

**149** Let's see: before that, before moving my body and my mind from where the roots don't go down, don't grasp the earth, let's go backward, let's go back to what calls us, wins us, buys us and sells us.

**150** Because, really, what would the past be without the audacious ones who dare to reinvent it? Re-invent it. Invent again what's already there: a fantasy. A lie, a story created to offer happiness, diversion, to the omnipotence of certain children that inhabit us. But nothing more. Because, what, from any past, could be so dead that it doesn't inhabit each drop of the present? What could be so buried? What could have disintegrated so much into what emptiness? What could have vanished to such an extent?

**151** That history, which in other circumstances one might dare to write with a capital letter, which almost doesn't perceive the movement of events on skates, the one thought up, imagined, plotted and produced, put in motion by human brains, hands, legs and sexual organs, enjoys certain privileges. Among them, the permission that the passage of time gives it to feed on living beings. Sucking them, chewing them, absorbing them.

One could ask oneself: does so much cannibalism have its origin in some urge for survival? Because it desperately razes. Because it exterminates. It annihilates and exterminates. Quietly or with much shouting. In succession or simultaneously.

At some point I'll have to reflect upon how history, for a period of more or less seventeen years, chewed up and swallowed my friend Juliana (who is Estela).

**152** When the sun peeks out around the sides of winter in Los Angeles, when it intercepts us along the wide avenues in the middle of the route that takes us to work in my shamefully white Toyota Corolla in good repair, when it confronts us through the windshield causing a sequence of burning and tears, when it announces to us that the rays take off rapidly in a straight line until they hit the skin of the world's inhabitants, it's lying: winter has no sides; there are no white Toyota Corollas in good repair; nothing can make us cry. And, above all, the rays of the sun do not reach us in a straight line. In reality they leave the fire in a constant explosion that sends them shaking, snaking, shivering with uneasiness, with uncertainty, tangling themselves one upon another, bumping, fighting for their own space, in order to reach us, to reach me, exhausted, without definition, irritated, irritating, with a desire to lie down and sleep, with a desire to see me lie down and sleep.

**153** Like when halfway through the twentieth century (the one that just left us, sorrowfully, reproaching us for having neither comprehended nor interpreted it), the nylon stockings of our mothers ran and had to be taken to the lady across the street, the one who stitched them up. One by one, from down below to the upper seam. With that kind of delicate, little crochet needle. That's how you stitch up the runs of the so-called past, hooking them one onto the other, meticulously and purposefully, toward the province of the present. To connect with the vibrations of today.

**154** I ask of you, savage earth that blackens the bottoms of my feet, a certain tolerance. I remind you, my dear, that one doesn't learn to levitate in a few attempts, however vigorous.

**155** Juliana, with the sweet wide-set eyes the color of the sky, had arrived with another sixty-nine women, myself among them, at the Villa Devoto prison, comfortably situated in the neighborhood of the same name in Buenos Aires. She had been shackled, just like the rest, to the empty floor of the military plane that transferred us from the basement of the Rosario Police Station. She had been stripped for a surprising medical examination upon being admitted to the new prison, like all the rest. She'd been assigned to the ward with a group of twenty-nine others, a group that included myself. All this after she'd passed through the hands of the requisite torturers who'd tried to obtain information pertinent to her political activities, and those of who knows how many others, always availing themselves of the not necessarily infallible methods of the electric cattle prod, blows expertly dealt upon the sensitive regions of the body, and gang rape. Stuff like that. That's the short version, just to give you some context.

And so, having arrived at ward 31, while at least three were vomiting loudly trying to rid themselves of the emotional and physical offences we'd suffered in the course of the transfer and its details, while others looked for a way to let prisoners in the other wards on the floor know we'd arrived like bats in a new attic, to establish contact and let them know we were alive, Juliana had become some kind of *rosca de reyes* deposited on the innermost bed of our shiny new dwelling place. And she shook with sobs that, in their own rhythm and harmony were analogous, in their function, to the synchronized vomiting taking place in the row of three latrines along the end of the ward.

Well, I thought, not having decided whether to vomit or not and being unsure about the existence of the other wards, thanks to that infallible sense of direction that life never gave me, I better go over to her and find out what's going on. So, sitting down on the edge of the bed that she'd adopted as her own, I stayed there looking at her and not a single comforting or inspiring word managed to emerge from amidst the racket, from among the tumult that was my thoughts.

Or the lack of them. I remember the moment. I remember the moment, its hollows.

**156** I don't know if anyone has come to any conclusion regarding the age-old argument as to whether the brain, in a conscious state, can really go blank. In other words, without words. But the truth is, that instant is not a fantasy. And it can be deadly.

**157** There is no way to escape the catastrophe that accompanies the death of the word, even if that death is transitory. Even though it paves the way for future accumulation and prodigality without limits (which is also fleeting, truth be told). There's no way to escape the drama when the word decides to take a goddamn vacation. Fatal invasion of simultaneous snows.

**158** I remember the moment, its hollows, its passageways to an unrecognizable temperature, inexpressible. And I remember myself, circulating through them until contact with the combination of the perfect wool blanket made for the worst Argentine winter and the furious heat of the Buenos Aires summer gave me back the ability to emit sounds. I could have used that combination, that contrast, to explode out of all proportion, in screams of rage and impotence, or to ask some stupid question of Juliana (whose name I still didn't know) that might help her to recover her also misdirected, derailed word. But no. I didn't say anything. And, besides, Juliana had decided to cry herself to sleep.

**159** Walking, as you should, on the wild-wild side.

**160** And so now, in January of 2000, I ask myself questions. Even though from my childhood up until my imprisonment my literary themes tended toward the social, the ideological, those of human weakness, if prison and exile hadn't existed, what would have been my themes, other than the various obsessions that I return to so frequently?

**161** And now a non-question. An affirmation: does the climate change the themes? Do the themes change with the changing climate? Do the themes change the mood? Does the mood change the themes? Does the limpid night become embedded in the heart of those who steadily watch the stars from whatever terrace or mountaintop of this world?

**162** And to prove that the supposed past merges with the present until it disappears completely in it, let's continue with Juliana.

Prison kept us together for years, until her release. Six months after it, came mine. Supervised. And her supervised release and my supervised release kept us together through the ups and downs of the city of Rosario, for another year and a half. Simple, isn't it? Here's the short version in a list: cafés, conversations, reminiscences, problems finding work because of being subversives, work, friends, ex-prisoners (women and men), threats from the *milicos*, being followed in the streets, being called to the police station and the Second Army Command Headquarters, friends helping you find work, more work, more lack of work, more friends, more cafés, movies, theater, more being followed, and once in a while giving in to the need for affection that would, in the future, make Juliana feel like the worst cretin in the world, but not me.

**163** That's why the planet spins so much. So that it all gets mixed up in a marbled background where it's impossible to distinguish details or differences. Spinning and spinning, so feelings can't be distinguished from political leanings. Desires from likes. Joys from guilt. Love from worry. Sacrifices from impulses. The need to feel that you're back in the world of the living and you're one of them, part of the immorality.

**164** The dream of the seventeen traveling oceans moving in parallel directions, their waters shaking with desperation in their depths until they become sublime and permanent conflagrations, is not coincidental. Its recurring nature isn't surprising. The images' insistence on reappearing and standing vigil during breakfast, lunch, during strolls around the city, in the middle of a break, work hours, get-togethers with friends, the time you spend taking stock at the end of the day, is nothing more than their caprice, forcing us to see that the potential for change is virtually infinite. The dream of the seventeen traveling oceans stirring their fires as if nothing more existed. As if nothing more.

**165** So the roles were assigned, more or less, and Juliana, apparently, got to be the less resistant of the two, while an abiding friendship was forged minute by minute by the blows of the jailers on the bars of our doors that woke us every morning, by our daily dealings with death, by the solidarity and the disagreements, and by the explosion of overwhelming beauty at sundown each day, which without any doubt, or at least none that we'd admit to, we would see again some day.

Until the year 1978, the year of liberty for many of us. When they opened the doors of Villa Devoto, to Juliana on July 9th and to me on December 24th. Dates on which unfortunately neither her husband nor my *compañero*, the one with the desperate and transparent eyes, had any doors open to them, none of any color or texture or volume or weight or size.

**166** Not to them, and not to so many others.

**167** And love? Let's try to treat this delicately, shall we? Let's skip the irony. And let's do without the snickering and snide remarks from the eternally disillusioned. Putting cynicism to one side, though it's tempting at times, I admit it. Little by little. Controlling the inclination, the slight pressure, almost impossible to detect, of the inside of the top lip against the left canine that, if it could be seen, would reveal the tiniest bit of sarcasm. Very watered down, of course, by the waterfall of ideas, like a pinch of paprika in the great stewpot that feeds the twenty-seven people who come for Sunday dinner.

And in addition, be careful of the incongruencies.

Because the truth is that you love so much. Everything is done out of love for something. Or out of lack of love. Or out of stupidity.

What really ends up being unnecessary is the more or less habitual question about the nature of things, that we should learn not to ask ourselves. For example: What is this? What is that? What is beyond? What is love?

Because it isn't anything. Love isn't anything. And if it is something, it's nothing more than a strange epileptic hodgepodge of hormonal tremors and the terror of walking lost along the deserted avenue of time. Isn't it? Who has another take on it, honestly? And could it be that you yourself have another take on it?

But, in spite of everything, you love. You love so much. And you do things that would be inconceivable if they hadn't been compelled by love. Or by the need to be loved, which is another form of love.

When you recover the means of functioning in certain ways, when you take the bus again, or buy a sandwich, or go see a movie (not to say that you have gotten your freedom back because that's a lie: no one gets their freedom back) you also explode – careful now: don't take this axiom literally – with love. But more than anything you experience a savage and amusing, almost comical, desire to be loved. And there's no way to satisfy it without letting yourself be loved. Which, any way you look at it, has a whole avalanche of consequences. Some succumb to the pure beauty of a man, as happened to sweet Juliana. Others get confused by the temptation to accumulate new experiences, as happened to me. But these two conditions which naturally occur in some people, which are enjoyed by others, and which some lack, are not as vain as certain infallible beings would like to believe (in order to spread the blame around). Beauty is love. Sex is love. Everything desirable is love. And of course our *compañeros*, husbands, boyfriends, prisoners, were the love – that would be awaiting when they returned to the street – and it wasn't that we were forgetting such a privilege, of course not.

**168** No, we weren't forgetting anything. Neither how long it would take to perceive those small pimple-like things piling up on the back of our necks, nor the surprise that comes with the realization that they are eyes, and that with those eyes comes the potential to use them.

And so it goes.

**169** Not anything. We don't even forget what we haven't seen. What's hard to believe. What's finally accepted. What was just incorporated into our muscular tissue. How to let it go less (or more) expeditiously, with what you hope would alleviate but which does little more than accentuate the shades of horror: a cushy sofa and a John Grisham novel.

**170** So let's take a leap and return to Juliana. Who was traveling through the air on her way to Aubervilliers, a neighborhood or town on the outskirts of Paris. With her husband, recently rescued from the schizophrenia of the Argentine cells.

Light fragments from the explosion, splinters of the dusk.

And Juliana, headstrong and volatile, dedicated since the instant of the plane's glorious arrival to the oh-so-noble task of recovering her relationship with Vicente. Reasonable. That's how things should be done. The paths of original love should take their course. The interruption hadn't been caused by either of them. It had come from elsewhere, external and scarcely anticipated. And now everything was left behind: Rosario. The beautiful man who'd reminded her that she was alive. Family: father, sisters, mother, in-laws, cousins. The group of friends. And those are only the human elements. And so off she went, seated next to her husband, ex-political prisoner, on an Air France flight. Most likely packed in like sardines between a fat lady who occupied the aisle seat (so she wouldn't rub her behind into some other passenger's nose with every trip to the bathroom) and Vicente who, as a man who'd just been liberated from the horror, deserved the window seat.

Meanwhile I was in Los Angeles, perceiving a third part of it all, absorbed by the facts that implicated the Greek green grocer, making an effort to decipher the conglomeration of stars in the new sky, and waiting, attentively, for signs of Juliana's landing in Paris.

**171** Because in life things have to happen. Because we aren't, some of us, content to be without events. And if they don't appear from other dimensions, you simply have to make them happen.

**172** Could it be that, in the end, this existence we endure is a factory of events, one that all of us who wish to can use to whatever extent is necessary to confront our own boredom? Well, I mean, not all of us have a phobia of tedium. A lot of people are bored, and they love it. They just sit there, looking out into space, at specks of dust in the air, with no conflict at all.

**173** And so Juliana (Doot da-doo da-doo . . .) began to walk through Paris and its environs. She walked and she walked until she learned French. She walked and walked, and each day picked up a little more of the reality that surrounded and contained her. She walked, while she barely resisted the attacks of Vicente, who was dying to get a detailed confession out of her, about the beautiful man who'd reminded her she was alive. All these details, at first pieced together in the open afternoons of Los Angeles, then later on the paved and unpaved streets of Mexico City. So many letters from Aubervilliers. All of them pages and pages long.

Ultimately, Vicente decided that the only way to convince his wife (now the mother of his first-born son) that she could talk without risk was to promise her that nothing would change between them. Because he was magnanimous, disinterested, and, more than anything, perfectly capable of understanding it all, including Juliana's need, like that of any ex-prisoner (meaning me) for affection, for sex, for companionship, after everything we'd been through, after all the profound disagreements that destiny had thrown at us, after all the unjust blows life had dealt, our lives being worse than any Latin American soap opera, but real, goddamn it, real, and I'm going to understand you completely, because besides, I'm warning you, I'm not willing to lose you, we have a child and hope to have more, and my love for you and our family can't be compared to anything, we haven't gotten this far just to throw it all out the window as if we could just be born all over again and besides who wants to be born again, we deserve to be who we are, and come on, to keep being proud of ourselves, of our ability to understand each other, of being, let's be clear here, different, of tolerating life's inconveniences, and as for me I'm not like some of those other sexist, spoiled petit bourgeois men out there, accustomed to getting whatever they want by whatever means, me who, by unfortunate circumstance, let his woman's crotch slip from my hands, just one of those things, an accident, one of many that occur in the course of the complex, heroic, never-ending, and indispensable job of changing the world. Do you understand me, my love? Who better than I? Who better to listen to you, to offer you my shoulder, to listen to and make sense of your anguish, your feelings of guilt, your, how can I say this, true desires? I am your *compañero*. I am the man that you decided to join your destiny to. I'm not trying to say that if, as the years pass, and things don't go well between us we're obliged to stay together, forcing ourselves, as if marriage were some kind sport and staying together were the Olympics. No. But we're an enormous distance from that eventuality. I love you, never in all my years in jail did I stop thinking of you even for an instant, your picture went through all kinds of struggles and I always managed to save it from the clutches of the enemy, don't ask me how I managed to keep it with me after some extreme measures that left me with a broken body, that put me in solitary confinement. Such were my ways of loving you, of remembering you. Of maintaining make-believe encounters with you. Such were my ways of surviving. But no, don't cry, Juliana. There's no reason to cry. Here we are, now. And you can count on me. I understand, and I'm ready to understand so much more, every detail of your most intimate needs. How can I not understand, my dear? Don't you think I felt the same urges? The only difference, of course completely circumstantial, was the fact that the *milicos* gave you freedom first. And well, what are we going to do? At least Sara got out right after you and you two could keep each other company. It could have happened the other way around. Right? I could have gotten out before you, and who knows how things might have happened. No, don't cry. I can't bear to see a woman cry, especially you. Besides you're going to wake the kid.

Tell me if what I'm saying isn't true. Who knows if I would have had the presence of mind to practice celibacy while I waited for you? Sex is as necessary as any other natural function of our bodies, Juliana. We're not discovering America here. I recognize I'm not saying anything brilliant. You have to fuck. That's all there is to it. And we already had to abstain too long. You shouldn't feel bad. We're human beings aren't we? With what right, and on what basis, am I suddenly going to start expecting you to be the Virgin Mary? Because, my dear, we both know that you always liked it. And, besides, who the hell doesn't like a little bit of the in-and-out? C'mon, c'mon don't be like that. Have a sense of humor. We have enough to deal with already, so let's not make this bigger than it is. We have enough ahead of us. So much to overcome, build, rebuild and rehabilitate. Combine that with all the baggage from our recent past. And our not-so-recent past. What I mean to say is, our childhoods. They weren't the worst, mind you, but they weren't any barrel of laughs either. And anyway, I'm telling you, there are many ways to see this: why should a guy like me – or a woman like you – get caught up in this, or in any other kind of triviality? If you just think for a moment about who we are, you're going to realize what I'm trying to tell you. We're not your average people. We belong to an exceptional group. We, Juliana, awaken to life with eyes sensitive to what's happening in this world. We knew from the beginning of our days that the world needed us, that it had serious expectations of us. We understood that we had a job to do, and that to take it upon us, to accept such a challenge, was to run a great risk. People like us, who see life from that perspective, who don't hesitate to give priority to the group, to the society in which they live, putting aside any petty or egotistical need, who decide that they themselves only matter in the context of fighting for the good of others, people who are capable of choosing greatness to that extent, greatness of spirit, a spirit of sacrifice, would they give in to the foolishness, to the pettiness, to the small-mindedness, of reducing themselves to vulgar, miserable, jealousy? How could I not understand that another being, a human being, the human race, has weaknesses? This is the thing: he who is willing to give his life for the betterment of others, of his community, only feels love for it. I am one of those. I went through that experience in jail because I feel love for humanity. And you're part of that humanity. How could I not understand you? On top of that we've been in love for years, and at this moment in our lives you're nursing a new being who I engendered in your body, and who also belongs to that same humanity. Do you realize what I am trying to say to you? Faced with such a reality, Juliana, don't think that I'll be dissuaded by mean-spirited considerations, typical of insensitive and dirty minds. No. Don't worry. I'm a noble soul. You can confide in me. You can lean on my shoulder and let yourself rest there. You can let go, little by little, putting aside the rigidity of your body and spirit. And confide. We are no longer in jail, that period of torture is over, we are in another country, on another continent, on another side of the world. We are safe. Protected. This place defends us and gives us the opportunity to develop who we are. It is no longer necessary to invest all our energies to construct monstrous, brutal defense mechanisms. Now let us construct, let us reconstruct, the relationship we always desired but for which the enemy gave us neither the required space nor time. Come here. Give me a hug. Tell me all about it. Tell me how you lived through so much pain. How the solidarity of your *compañeras* in jail helped you to survive. Hold me, Juliana. There, there, my love. There, there. Tell me again how Sara's friendship gave you the support you needed to confront the loneliness after jail, the strength to work, the energy to visit me when I was still a prisoner, the wherewithal to endure the frustration of needing to be with me and being unable, the intelligence to understand that the attraction you might feel for another man had nothing to do with a lack of love for me. Juliana, my dear, let's talk. I understand everything. Tell me all about it. Now, more than ever, we are part of life. We are no longer separated. We have won the battle. Now no one will destroy what we build with our love, and with the desire that we nourish to strengthen it, with the experience that life has offered and that we have accepted. Come now, my love. Lay down beside me and tell me everything. Come now. Don't cry.

**174** Aha. Yes. Exactly. This is why it's always a good idea to keep those fluttering eyes on our neck wide open. Open. And clean, clean. And, every once in a while, make them up a bit. A little shadow on the lids, some mascara. Never, ever, abandon them, or underestimate their importance. Nor assume that their visual acuity is any less than that of the eyes that shine beneath our brows.

**175** And if suddenly something starts to itch, maybe, to annoy you, somewhere on your elbow, maybe it's the climate, a little dry sometimes, isn't it? Scratch it with care. Without hurting it. Especially if you feel a little bump that you hadn't noticed before. Or two.

**176** That we hadn't noticed before. That we hadn't noticed before. What anxiety, what darkenings that grow so large inside us, what compulsion to trap all light inside our mind, any vestiges of light, when we finally begin to measure the extent of everything we hadn't noticed before.

**177** Of all the things we might be missing now. That we won't notice in the future. And the verbs. You know? Conjugation is such a difficult part of learning a new language. So many nuances in looks, in gestures, in desires, in the ways of verifying meanings. Of corroborating loves. Love affairs. Displays of courage, of heroism, of everyday cowardice. The list of little white lies.

So intricate, it would seem, the language of far away.

**178** You ask yourself if it wouldn't be better to return. To return to your own river. On whose sandy shores the sun's humidities have been penetrating and darkening the pores of almost all your body for years. To the same old corner. The one with the café, half a block from the college where you showed off the ability to discover that natural phenomenon that we sometimes call first love. To your own sky. The one that imposes limits, designs and forms that we live with and for. To the ice cream parlor in the center of town, where the *dulce de leche* with chocolate chips is as unbeatable as it is inevitable. To the hand of your first boyfriend. To the secrets shared by your first friend. To the nausea brought on by the sight of your first dead cat, spread out and stretched, rubbed flat by a succession of automobiles on the gray city street.

You ask yourself if it wouldn't be better to return. To that red cotton dress with the small and medium-sized flowers of different blues, fitted and sleeveless, that defied all your efforts to appear discreet and modest in front of your friends. To return to your own rains, the ones that fall out of control, without any peace, incapable of enjoying the action that busies them. Your own rains. Heavy. Solid. Opaque. That sometimes, when they go, leave behind some bright spots.

Your first cigarette. Half-smoked, or less, at nine years old, swiped from your chain-smoking father's pack, that cigarette that left you with blood-stained bronchial tubes for a month, and with your mother and father's shouts reverberating through the neural pathways of your tender, sticky brain.

To your first real lie. To return to your first lie and sit down with it. Sit down with all its enormity, face to face, and ask it, trying to comprehend something of its origins and its illusions.

Would it be better to return, you ask yourself.

**179** To return. To return. To where?

**180** To your own spring. To the clever tricks of a winter that, with all the absurdity of its dampness and the per-petual nausea of its irreversible cold, still, and you have yet to figure out how, manages to be, every so often, something you miss. To the excessive clear-sightedness of the doves in the plaza, who never have any doubt about when to take off on their short flights and when to land and eat the old crumbs.

**181** And this is no joking matter. When the question arises, it demands an answer.

**182** No, I'm not crying. No. Or yes, yes I'm crying, but from emotion. From knowing that I can confide in you and finally remove this weight that dictates every movement of my life. Because, you know what? I don't decide anything. My entire existence is in the hands of this enormity that I drag around. No, not the baby, Vicente, my dear. What are you saying? No. The baby is my one and only relief. I'm talking about what you want to know. I know how difficult it will be for you to listen to what I'm going to tell you. But you're right, we have to talk about it all, because all that matters is that we're alive, that we're on the other side of the world, and that we're a family. A family that has to be saved.

Look, the only thing I ask is that you believe me. I'm going to tell you the details that are so anguishing to you, but it's important that you understand that there aren't so many and they're not so interesting. The main thing is obvious: it was so hard to find a job. You know that as well as I do. You go, you fill out an application, they interview you once, everything seems to go great, and you come back the following week to find out if they've given you the job or not. And you're convinced they did because everything couldn't have gone better. And you get there, and it turns out that the faces have changed. You can't even imagine. The same people, but now they're made of ice. Ice cold. After you go through this five, six times, there's no doubt about what's happening: they say the same thing to you, every time, as if they'd all memorized the same lesson: Honey, you're the best candidate for the job. Perfect. Divine. No one like you. With all the experience you have, on top of such an ideal situa-

tion, you're pretty, no kids, still young, you've got everything in your favor. But the one problem you have is the
killer: a previous record. You were imprisoned for subversive activities. So I can't give you the job. And I'm
telling you right now that it's not going to be easy to find
a job. You want the truth? It would be a miracle. No one
wants terrorists anywhere. And, let me tell you, even if I
did decide to give you the job, in less than an hour the
*milicos* or the police would issue a summons and make me
fire you. Or they'd threaten to close me down. Or they'd
kill me in the street. Right here. I'll give you some advice:
hop a plane and go far away. The best thing you could do
is to leave the country. No one wants subversives here.
You're a hot potato. Better to start over somewhere else.
I'm telling you the truth.

   That's how it was, Vic. Time after time. You were
still a prisoner, and you were in the same situation that
I'd been in just a little while before. Being a prisoner was
hell. But being outside navigating the swampy rivers of
that disintegrated society wasn't like being free. It was
another version of the same hell. You felt desperate when
nobody would give you a job and you couldn't, didn't
want to, depend on your family. To put them in danger, to
take from their mouths the bread they'd worked so hard
to earn. You leapt straight from jail to the plane and did-
n't see any of it. You have no idea what those two years of
"liberty" were like for me. For me and for all the other
"liberated". It was a circle. A horrible, vicious circle that
only your imagination could stop once in a while. And you
know I'm not very imaginative.

   And so there was this guy, the cousin of a new friend
of my sister, and what do I know, my sister told him about
what happened, he was moved, I guess, Vic. I don't know.
The thing is that he managed a downtown branch of
Monteleone, the appliance business. And he needed a sec-
retary. He interviewed me and he hired me. Let's just say

he was the miracle that all those sons of bitches talked about, the ones who weren't willing to produce any miracles of their own. And so day by day he started asking me questions about everything that had happened: jail, torture, and politics, which were Greek to him. He showed interest and sensitivity. Interest and affection. I needed them both. I needed them a lot. You can't imagine how much. One day, in the office, he told me something about a boy who'd survived torture in the Information Service. We talked about it and I was left with the impression that I'd seen that boy, that they'd been torturing him at the same time as me, in the room next door. He described him and it was as if I knew him perfectly. And something gave inside me. I don't know what happened to me, but I relived everything from up close. My tears flowed. That was the beginning. Then I lost myself in loud sobs and suddenly I realized that I couldn't stop. It was terribly embarrassing, but at the same time I'd lost control of my emotions and I couldn't find a way to pull myself together. He embraced me, just like anyone with a modicum of understanding would do. And that's how it began.

And he was a beautiful guy. Good looking. Vic, you don't know what a huge relief it is to be able to tell you this. Thanks for everything. Seriously. He was, he is a very beautiful guy physically. With big, black, deep eyes. Tall, with a bright and easy smile. Way too cognizant of his beauty, though. But you know, sometimes in life that helps: to be handsome, and to know you're handsome. But in his case it made him fickle. That's it. We ended up in bed because, arrogant or not, he understood me. He picked up on my underlying sensitivity, and was willing to make me feel good. Or at least to try. We talked a lot. We talked a lot about you. Hours and hours, we spent, him asking me about jail and politics, things that had never interested him before. And me asking him how he saw things from the outside, from his perspective, of course. A perspective that in the beginning wasn't clear to me, but that little by little became so. He was no idiot. We talked about my future with you. About the children that you and I would have. About this baby that we have now, that I knew we would have. You see. And he never got angry or jealous. We knew perfectly well that you were my *compañero*, my love, my everything. That was never up for discussion. He asked me questions about you, about your activism (never anything that he, not being aware of these kinds of things, realized you should never ask or know), about your character, all very reverently. He never felt guilty about occupying a place that didn't belong to him, about taking something from you, or usurping your space, because he knew that none of it belonged to him to begin with. He had a lot of respect, a lot of generosity, a lot of mental openness in his attitude. If it were any other way I wouldn't have been able to even get near him.

Don't look at me like that. Why are you looking at me like that? I know you understand. Or don't you? Isn't this our son? I didn't have a child with him. Right? This should tell you something, I suppose.

Vicente, the last thing I ever wanted was for things to go like this. I dreamt that we would both be given liberty on the same day, at the same moment. For years nourishing that desire and those images. Giving them forms, movements, speeds, and different colors every time. Creating different intensities, sharpnesses, of that first glance of yours after years. Trying out temperatures of the hands that you were going to touch me with, caress me with. The same as you. Just like you did every day and night in the rare instances of peace and solitude. Just like we all did. And, well, it didn't happen. It went another way. It's not like we hadn't considered this other possibility, but we fantasized so much about the ideal scenario, about what didn't turn out to be. But the form that life gives to things can be corrected. Adulterated. It depends on how you see them. We're doing that now. Erasing and redoing. We have to be careful though. We can't go making holes in the paper by erasing too hard. What we can't erase, Vic, we'll have to dissolve: talking, fighting, crying. Quite a job, my love. But you and I were never afraid of work.

And he, he is in the past. The remote past. He is a friend. A good friend. Who decided to take a great risk by giving me a job when there was a line of hundreds of girls younger than I, quicker, and without the subversive magnet to attract the *milicos* to his business or his life. This in the worst moments of the country's history. He, with those immense pupils, that in reality weren't pupils at all but charcoal irises, charred, swimming on the surface of a white sea, a drastic, near audible and resounding contrast with his dark and dense eyelashes, his thick eyebrows giving a strategic frame to his whole face, his great big smile that tempted you to open your mouth and tell every last thing that you might be hiding in your intestines, he, with his height and long fingers, retained only the status of friend. The kind of friend who falls into the category of unforgettable.

That's how things go. And you're my *compañero*. My husband. And the father of my son. And you're the person by whose side I will cross from one end to the other, this domain of estrangement, alterations, fantasies, dejection, solidarity, absurdities, missteps, lessons learned, loneliness, hallucinations, contempt, some happiness, surprises, anguish and heartrending grief that sometime someone for some reason decided to christen exile. At your side. And no one else's. What you fear so much, Vic, is in the past. It belongs to a time that has careened away from me at a dizzying speed. I'm light years away from all that. I'd almost say I don't recognize my own face. I look in the mirror, on certain days, and there I find a Juliana I can't possibly talk to, keep up a dialogue with. My hair doesn't shine. The skin on my face is dry, porous. And forget about the light that used to leap in my eyes for some reason I can't explain. Ciao. Gone. It must have found a place on some other woman's face. Or man's. I don't know. I'm telling you: I feel like a very different person. I feel it clearly. A person who would be completely foreign to the one from a year ago, who relearned liberty with the enthusiasm of someone who'd never experienced it before.

And to prove to you that what I'm saying is true I am going to do something that causes me a kind of pain I've never known: I'm going to write to Sara. Like I always do. She'll get the letter from her Mexican postman who knocks on her door quite often these days thanks to me, and others, in her house on Revolución in the capital, and she'll open it with the same excitement as always. And as she begins to read it she won't understand much. And halfway through she'll understand less, and by the end she won't believe what I, her soul mate, her friend Juliana, her sister through all of life's ups and downs, is telling her in its probably ten or more pages. And what I will be telling her is that I need to cut my ties to the past. That those times in Rosario when the two of us lived in disorientation, missing our *compañeros*, are behind us. That I want you to feel that I'm not dragging my anguish with me, nor my desires, nor doubts. That you and this son of ours occupy my whole life, and so that I can concentrate completely on you and on him, she will have to stop writing to me. I'm going to declare that the letter she is reading is my last one. I am going to explain everything to her. I am going to tell her that I know that I'm causing her pain. I am going to say that I am terribly sorry for what I did and that, out of either cowardice or shame, I do not want to speak about it again. I am going to tell her that I love you. In my own way, one that doesn't have to be the same as other people, that everyone else in the world must have, I suppose, their own way of being in love, or of loving, or of feeling affection, but I love you, and I'm determined to save our relationship. I'm going to tell her that you have always loved me and that you show it to me every moment. I am also going to tell her, maybe in the middle of a crying jag like I'm having right now, that it hurts me so to interrupt our communications at a time when all I really want is to know every detail about her pregnancy, about her growing belly, just like she knew everything about mine. It hurts me deeply. I'm going to tell her that when you and I have cleared everything up and we're ready to share our emotions with other people, that I'll write to her again.

What's happening? What's going on? Why are you looking at me that way? You're looking at me as if you were trying to find the most vulnerable place on my body to stick me with a knife. Vic, wait. Where are you going? What are you going to do? I understand how you feel. I understand everything that must be bothering you. But we've been talking about understanding and patience. Haven't we? Why are you taking those books? Where are you going? It's two in the morning. Don't make so much noise. You're going to wake up the baby and it's not time for him to eat yet. Please. Don't go. What are you going to do? Please, don't go. Stay here. Vic, please. Close the door slowly then. Don't slam it.

**183** There are so many simultaneous stories being told, building upon each other like apartments in the downtown of some large, complex city, sprawling and chaotic. In the same way that forests weave themselves together day by day, becoming entangled and overgrown. So many stories growing and suffocating one another. So many, so why not add one more: the story of desolation.

**184** The story of the desolation of sweet Juliana of Aubervilliers, a neighborhood or town on the outskirts of Paris, with a happy, healthy son, who busily consumed her energies by way of her two, voluminous tits. Cast aside by her husband, more emotionally than economically, and punished with vigor and enthusiasm by each of her own, various, phantoms, not to mention Vicente's, and the baby's, because no one's exempt from phantoms, and let's not forget to feed them, to offer them exotic, gourmet foods (like cockroaches bathed in chocolate, since it's important to remember that cockroaches are the protein of the future, with humanity multiplying as it is, with so many extra bogymen) to keep toys handy so they can entertain themselves, so that they'll stay more or less quiet, but always be there. Ready when they are called upon to act.

And please, please, don't let them diminish, don't let them escape from me. Don't let them destroy me through their absence. Don't let them empty me. Don't let them take away who I am. I need my shadows to protect me. I need my phantoms to help me pay for my guilt. And I need to weep to eliminate the toxins created by pain.

**185** You go away and then return. You come back so many times you know you could walk away from any survival situation virtually unscathed. You try and try to create the sensation of never having died. Of never having died before this time. Of a succession of deaths instead of a final, complete and illusory death awaiting us. Because the fact is that behind every departure, even when you're not paying much attention, you can perceive a return peering out at you, making its presence felt, determined not to interfere with the laws of pendular motion. We've been dying so much. So energetically. We've been returning to life, rebounding off the wall that we've been executed against so many times, so energetically. And you've grown eyes in the orifice of each Ithaca rifle or canon, so energetically. Eyes that need no help from glasses to demonstrate their enormous visual acuity.

We leave, we come back, repeating the departures and the returns, the agonies, comas, the muffled cackles of those addicted to the vertigo of the swing, the swing in the park with the super-strong iron chain and the broken link, open, always about to let the seat fall.

There are so many exiles. And we've been exiling ourselves every day and every night, racking up so many forced retreats, and as many voluntary ones as returns. And every return is another exile, another one transporting us toward the next return, the next exile.

At the kitchen table in the apartment where I live in Los Angeles I slowly eat a fresh, colorful salad, expertly seasoned in Buenos Aires. I eat it in Buenos Aires and I enjoy it in Los Angeles, the lettuce bought at the green grocer across the street from the house where I was arrested in Rosario, the one I shared with my *compañero*, that one with the terrible eyes. The vinegar and the tomato and maybe the cucumber, quickly picked out at the supermarket near the apartment where David paraded his obsessions, in the argentinized Torres de Mixcoac in Mexico City. The black olives pitted in some green Californian valley, probably around Santa Barbara, the extra-virgin olive oil produced in Rosario, and I chew my salad in Rosario and I swallow it in Los Angeles and I digest it in Cuernavaca and my body assimilates it in Mexico City and I prepare it in Buenos Aires and I enjoy it again in my own environs. On the outskirts, not the central point, precisely, of my sensibilities.

**186** And the more eyes the more phantoms. Right?

**187** Seated, seated on an overstuffed jet-black velvet sofa, defiant, I was reading. More precisely, I was making a valiant effort to try to read some of Chomsky's ideas. I wasn't uncomfortable. My legs were even stretched out and relaxed. But there was something there that impeded the perfection of the moment. It wasn't easily definable. My glasses weren't bothering me, because I didn't wear glasses and didn't need them. My hair wasn't caught on anything: My head was sinking down since there was nothing in the springy darkness of the furniture to stop it. Everything seemed in perfect order. But there was something in the pit of my stomach. Or no. Maybe further down. In my belly. Or in my vagina? In my uterus? No. No. Further down. Behind. On my butt. On the left cheek. Something had bitten me. I scratched. Damn it. Anyone would say what I was feeling was a hard-boiled egg that was pushing its way out for some reason. Who knows what nature will come up with next?

**188** No surprise. Even that is possible when your body has been exiled. Your mind. Your bones. Exiled.

**189** It's only a matter of scratching. Because there's nothing else to do: it itches, that's all there is to it. The only thing you have to keep in mind is that it's better not to do it any harm. Given everything you've been through it wouldn't be a bad idea to imagine that it's a seductive, almond-shaped eye (instead of the aforementioned hard-boiled egg) that's in the process of acquiring form and color on the strange but well-traveled landscape of your behind. To keep enriching your own perspective. Your own view of the world. The beaten, altered cosmogony.

**190** And so it was, with elegant simplicity and without any practical complications, that I found out (if we can accept the idea that you never know what's going to happen a moment from now) that I had lost my friend Juliana. That was all there was to it: the letter arrived at the door of the house where I lived, I opened it, read it, and in an instant my mouth was full of Mexico City, and the pungent taste of decomposing fish. My belly was growing rapidly, and the cold tones that seized my tongue, my teeth, were diminishing slowly, all thanks to my best friend's sudden decision.

**191** And there was nothing more for seventeen years. I mean: from her, nothing more. Until one afternoon in 1999 when Juliana's urgent need for forgiveness was relayed via the U.S. Postal Service.

**192** A first impression is nothing more or less than a kidney punch, which, of all the ones you receive, leaves the deepest, bloodiest hole, full of snakes and mysteries.

**193** A first impression can be, among other precious little things, a snake. And also a mystery.

**194** A snake can also be a mystery. And a mystery, a snake. A snake can be nothing more or less than a first impression and a mystery can be the same. And if a mystery is a first impression, the mystery, just like a bad liar, won't get very far. And if a first impression holds a mystery, that mystery can be as indecipherable as it is disagreeable, as depressing as it is eternal.


**195** Picking up where we left off with the story of events, events sometimes on roller skates, other times on a motorcycle and every once in a while on foot, the moment of remembering my own body had finally arrived. My own desire. A whole chain of desires. Listening to the appeals of this brain that luck stuck me with, accepting its need to separate lobes and furrows, unfolding all its parts, spreading out toward the unknown and exploding, scattering vibrations and beats, spattering its slivers, the daughters and granddaughters of the ancestral splinters. Those that would never return, will return, to the arms that cradled them. It was time to sniff the surrounding air and follow the rhythm of internal pulsations. The telegraphic tic-tic, not necessarily infallible. Telling me to board a plane. And fly.

And in the Mexico City International Airport a man I knew practically nothing about was waiting, different branchings of the tree of History were leading me to him: the possible denial of my petition for asylum in the United States, a need to break with the recent past, the current impossibility of returning to my own country, common professional/literary interests, a strong physical attraction, the inevitable suction of the unknown, a strong desire to share my daily life as an exile with the huge number of Argentine political refugees that were landing, hovering, entering, leaving, hiding themselves, standing out, making themselves hated, letting themselves be loved, working, getting dizzy, rising and falling between the Torres de Mixcoac and the Colonia Condesa, the Zona Rosa and the need to understand and to survive.

**196** And what about the different sounds of your urine compared to someone else's? Wouldn't it smell of a ghetto as well as ammonia? Of alienation, of yeast, of ammonia. Ghetto. As if we hadn't had enough. Please. Please. Not that it's easy, but let's open ourselves to the world. Open those private hours of the day and daybreak to whatever it may be that we hadn't allowed across our borders before. The borders we have made, that have made us and that we had never thought to open. I wonder: Is it possible? Would it be possible in a sudden burst of inspiration to open the orifices of the pores and admit new airs, different aromas, sound waves of varying decibels, new contacts to stimulate our movements, original dances, danced with yourself and with others? Does it sound feasible or is it just a feeble expression of desire, a delirium, the ravings of fatigue, of the undefeatable, endless exhaustion?

What is the newness that we yearn for? Why do we cultivate such difference?

**197** He was waiting and observing me from behind some glass wall while airport employees rummaged through luggage that was not in any conventional order anyway. I asked myself what he would be thinking when he detected in my face an attempt to appear calm, set among those features that give exiles their determined grimace, that tone, that special coloring to the skin, that recognizable muscle tension running back and forth across their faces, but especially between the eyes and the corners of the mouth, solidifying them into a single form, so exiled.

What would he be thinking. Oh well. And finally we hugged each other (I think we hugged) when I managed to pass the glass barrier. And we walked toward the street, where my new *compañero*'s car awaited.

**198** And now in the street, I mean on the sidewalk along the airport road, I stopped before crossing, because something, I don't know what, in the thickness of the air, the texture of the sounds, a sort of shadowing of grays and beiges that covered everything trapped me, tugged at my hair, gave me a warning. He was carrying my two suitcases, like two plump cheeks, and I had a bag. I put the bag on the ground and craned my head as far as possible in both directions. It wasn't necessary to look back: there was nothing more nor less than the airport. But it was necessary to look both ways. Slowly. Pausing, my head, my vision, at each billboard. For shampoo. Beer. Cigarettes. Supermarkets. Banks. A strange coherence began to disquiet me. The coherence had a color. That color established a uniformity that transformed my disquiet into alarm. The color was yellow. On each billboard a young blonde was peering out with a regal attitude, smiling with invasive and matching white teeth, with blue eyes like the California sky on a smog-free day. I looked at my new *compañero* with, let's just say, deep confusion. I picked the bag up off the ground, though it seemed I was still stuck to the sidewalk, and in that action my glance fell upon two very indigenous women walking along with three children who were as indigenous as they were. My neck hurt, all of a sudden. My neck was tense and surprised me by making a kind of singular, novel shriek. Novel and singular details always pop up when it's especially difficult to explain them. Anyway. I knew that I had to keep walking. My new *compañero*, a writer seventeen years my senior, a political exile in a country that had given refuge to so many South Americans, kept walking toward the car with my two suitcases. I started up again, with difficulty. Mental difficulty, that's how I'd describe it. And with my mouth open. It was December, and it wasn't cold, cold air didn't get in my mouth. So I decided to leave it open as long as I felt like it. I decided not to give in to pressure from anyone or anything. I decided I would close it when I was good and ready. My new *compañero* had already noticed something off in my expression, in what should have been my enormous joy at our meeting, and he formulated the question: What's wrong. But he didn't stop there. He continued: Now don't jump the gun, don't be so quick to judge. Don't be soooo Argentine. Give it all a chance. Now let's go. Let's go home. It's a long drive to Cuernavaca.

And so we went. But I already felt in my tendons and muscle fibers that circulating tickle that you also breathe, the one that invades when the light changes, when the physiognomy of the city starts to get distorted as night comes on, when what's coming is unpredictable, when before you, beside you, somewhere behind you, appears the certainty that what surrounds you has no certainty. The understanding that what moves around us and, in fact, contains us, is absence. A hole. A lie.

**199** Sometimes it rains, ladies and gentlemen. Cats and dogs.
And sometimes it doesn't.

**200** Gradually, to begin defining. What calls to us. Without anxiety. Trying to let the answers come naturally, with inner peace, almost with tenderness. Because you have to feel the caress. You have to remember that the caress exists and that you have to prepare yourself to receive it. To enjoy it. To let it work. Like conditioner for your hair. You have to not force the answers. They just appear. The answers find their own space. They open their own path. They appear, one day, and they are that caress, giving us satisfaction, relief from anguish. What calls to us. What called to us. What is it about each one of us. Is it so necessary to confirm our own existence? Is it so hard to live with doubt? What shrieking voices called to us. What echoes of those shouts resound in us each daybreak, in the middle of the sun's fluorescent contradiction, between its desperation to appear and the slowness with which it looses its most faraway flames. What inner roar woke us and found us ready to take the historical commotion and dance in it, shake ourselves in it, kiss each other in it? What question, what roar, still doesn't have an answer? Gradually. To begin defining. To begin defining the similarities between the nature of what emits the call and the material, the flesh it gets stuck in. And afterward, in the loneliness of a Sunday winter afternoon, having surmounted a polite lunch and the dishwashing that came after, with its sounds of china, glass, and rushing water, when the contours of the body decide to settle into the springy softness of the living room (someone's, anyone's, it doesn't matter), to return to the question without fear. To ask yourself again. Peacefully. What keeps us in the same circle. What permits us that space in which we coexist. What gives us the energy to recover that space if something takes it away from us, burns it down, tries to convince us that it was never ours in the first place. Let's think. What gives us the answer. What gives us that peace. And what will keep us returning to the same daily gathering, saving seats for each other, making sure that each of us have the opportunity to express our adhesion to the circle that contains us, the appreciation for what we have never ceased to be, for what has come to represent the reason for all our lives.

What is it that keeps us threaded like a necklace, looking at each other across the oceans, from one continent to the other, from one almost deserted island to another one, covered with unexpected vegetation, what brands us and leaves us branded, what makes us laugh ourselves silly in unison, what makes us wash our clothes with the same soap. What makes us use our fingers in that untransferable coded language. What calls to us. What has called us.

**201** Sometimes it rains. Even on the most enigmatic codes and the most multitudinous summons. And it's true that some people are born with an umbrella under their arm. And it's also true that when it rains cats and dogs they get so nervous that they can't bring themselves to open it. And what they do with an umbrella in that case, I don't know. It depends on their profession. A cook might come home soaked, take a hot shower, go to the kitchen and take out the lentil stew, perhaps with the umbrella. A doctor might use it as a stethoscope in an emergency, if someone slipped in the street and broke their leg in the middle of a torrential rain, or fractured their throat, or their pancreas. And a writer whose pencil got ruined in the rain could use it to write a novel that's halfway done and that he can't get out of his head until he finishes writing it and corrects it a hundred times until it is, for lack of a better word, perfect. Assuming the water didn't destroy the half-written manuscript. That fragile notebook that has to be protected. It has to be embraced, held tight against the chest, covered with kisses. It has to be promised many things.

**202** And don't even mention if, under the same meteorological conditions, you're a writer born with an umbrella that sometimes opens and sometimes doesn't, and if you are, all of a sudden, immersed in the day-to-day life of a country that is perceived of as an non-existent entity. And if, to complete the picture, the nonexistent country is no more nor less than one of the ones that so generously offers what we call exile. In other words: it's not to be disdained. Or given away. Or thrown in the garbage. Or sold. You are, literally, grateful for it. Over and over again.

**203** So, what is the fantasy of the writer exiled to some part of the world where the intimate and often evident desires of its inhabitants are represented by a blonde girl, a *güera*, who looks at them, so sure of herself, from an ad for a product that's intended to beautify their indigenous features? What is that writer who's faced with the almost infinite unfolding of realities and unrealities hidden between the leaves of the trees, between one word and the next in a conversation that's never defined? What does that writer do? Does he write? Does he observe, astonished as he is, the deployment of the sinuousities, the advance and concealment of signs, gestures, promises, smiles and threats? What does that writer dedicate his time and literary energy to, crushed as they are by the lonely, lockstep dance of the puppets of reality, by the ubiquitous artifice of the everyday?

**204** You think. You remember tones. Old tones, not quite assimilated all those years ago but heard successively, and intuited to be improbable, discordant. Inadequate. That bombastic voice, directed toward sullen, paternal ears. Let's buy her a fur coat, otter perhaps or mink. The finest quality. Something that will last her whole life. What are you laughing about? You don't think she'll ever wear it. Right? You think what she says about furs being disgusting is true. Well, what do I care? At least it's something that'll last her forever. End of discussion. Those sounds from perdurability that clatter and moo from one point in my brain to another. For her whole life. And the furniture: Provençal. It has to match. All of it Provençal. From the best wood. The kind that doesn't wear out. A noble, faithful material. Forever. We're not about to buy some piece of crap.

You remember those tones of the apocryphal, the unreal, and after the facial muscles, depending on their slight upward or downward movements, reflect the particular sensation experienced, the inventory begins: how many coats after that fur one, never worn. And the questions. Where did it end up. Who might be wearing it. And the books. Who might have burned them. Or read them. Or abandoned them at the dump. How many relocations. You make lists, long lists embellished with green, red, blue ball point pens, with very sharp lead pencils. Devoting one page to each household. Or two houses to a page, so as not to use so much paper, the blessed list, each house separated from the other by curls of curving, colored lines. Included, of course, are all the different prisons. And each place you've lived in every country of exile. How many coats you've bought. Not many, really. You've inherited many more from other exiles, the *adelantados*, the Álvar Núñez Cabeza de Vacas, those who first appeared in foreign lands completely deprived of the forever after, of that ancient, extemporaneous concept of perpetuity.

You think, from the armchair of the moment, the toilet of the moment in whatever country that shelters us, that the fragility of existence, just like the fragility of Provençal furniture, deserves all the dedication of a writer's mind to find the right words to evaluate it. To describe it. To meditate on it. The right, most opportune words to give such a fragile condition a sense of permanence. Of being infinite.

**205** I know, I found out about, the pain that can shatter the written word against a wall and leave it in fragments, splinters of blood and shrieks. I also found out about the pain of its own resurrection.

**206** Because sometimes the word survives.

Once upon a time, during those years of insanity and terror, there was a writer who wasn't assassinated. He wasn't assassinated because the day before the one on which the bullet, or cluster of bullets, was to hit him, either in the street, or in his house, he managed to squeeze onto a plane, to cross the widest ocean, and to settle in another country. In another country in this same world.

In other words, it wasn't so easy. Various countries afflicted him initially, that is until he decided that in one of them, chosen perhaps because of linguistic similarities, of communication or of heredity, the degree of distress would be lessened. And it was true. The writer had the proverbial clarity as to the importance of the word that can be expressed best: the one that belongs to your own language. And he accepted the reality that this was the one spot on the planet that would allow him to express his vital impulses through literature, besides expending the energy necessary for everyday things. He wouldn't have to compromise his mood with the processes and apocalypses of another language. He'd been right. He proved it. He could speak there, he could write, cry, enjoy a certain amount of sexual contentment, seduce, lie, express his most indispensable truths, all in his own language. He could, also, receive news of his country in the daily papers. And that was how it was. He settled in and began to acclimatize (for lack of a better word, because you need some way to express the phenomenon) himself. Among other things designed to ground him in reality, he got a dog. A puppy. And the puppy ran in circles around the writer's feet while he dug his elbows into the solidness of his oak desk. And one day news did in fact arrive from his country. That his son had just disappeared. That in his country the criminals in power had arrested his son and caused him to disappear. The son wasn't a boy. He was a young man, intelligent, sensitive, concerned about life. The writer became desperate. And because he hadn't yet reached the crying stage, he shouted. He shouted and he destroyed things, I suppose, he yelled insults and kicked in different directions. And the puppy at his feet received one of the kicks. One of the hard ones. Of the definitive ones. Such that at some point, almost without a moan, it stopped moving.

Years later the writer, in another part of the world, still exiled, cried, reliving the episode as one of most horrendous in his life.

The exile, dear writer, dear, is that chair upon which your buttocks tighten, strong and anxious, to give power and speed to the succession of letters that were being chosen, to the words that were being said. Exile is the puppy's rib, its femur, quivering, phosphorescent, in the not quite absolute darkness of our desperation. Exile is the calcium from those bones involuntarily giving themselves for the benefit of the earth, ground that isn't the ground we were born in, that's not the land that received, with or without indifference, the vibrations of our first steps, nor the dirt that absorbed our first urgent urination. Perhaps, yes maybe, our second, our third. In some cases our last. Exile, my friend, is that row of little colored papers that we make while we play pensively with our hands. Or the order, smallest to largest, that we give to the pencils on our desk that we use to outline our literary landings each day. Or that other row, the one of cadavers that we accumulate inside of us: the cadaver of tomato that we swallowed with the last of the *milanesa napolitana*. The cadaver of the daisy that, at any rate, lasted an awfully long time in the transparent glass vase. The cadaver of the last book we read, quiet now, so quiet on the shelf. The cadaver of the last book we wrote, recently finished, because that's the vertigo and the pain of the word producing itself, that's its trajectory: no sooner does it see the light of day than it rests, dead, like butterflies or like photos in the album they've been relegated to. Awaiting, who knows, some kind of resurrection. The cadaver of the son, the one of the idea said aloud, the one of the wood that was used to make the bed of your dreams. The one of the wood that made the headboard of the bed where you slept and wrote, where you massaged someone's ankles, someone's ear, and that was consumed down to the last splinter in a fire at some point.

Exile is the rebirth of the word that was conceived one day, do you remember? Looked at with affection, caressed, kissed with your teeth, sucked, destroyed in kisses, raped again and again, assassinated and deposited, finally, on the traditional whiteness, once free of guilt and pain, once innocent, virgin, once without signs of madness, without vestiges of shadows or loves. Exile is, also, and more than anything else, the reappearance of the word scrawled with all those bodily fluids.

Exile is your whole life. Each word that's inhabited us, that consumes us, that disperses us in the world and that accumulates us in the enormous receptacle of great desires, and that pours us out little by little, into glasses of different kinds, from which we will be consumed.

**207** That's the explanation for these (and so many other) words.

**208** How did we get here? Who brought us? Which among the many groups of phantoms that inhabit our arteries were molding our movements, what shadows, what whims of light came together to direct, to devise the tone of the question that we've been formulating? That's been pushing us to give it an answer. That's been worrying us so intensely. That's been destroying our patience. That offers an uncountable variety of possible answers every day, to the point that we have already forgotten the question.

**209** And how much pain does that forgetting bring, how much nostalgia. Especially if we can detect its eroding presence. How much bone does forgetfulness gnaw. How much hollow space does it leave.

**210** For that reason, so we can avoid the sadness and its many accoutrements, we're going to remember. Instant by instant. Profoundly. Down to the depths. To the edges of History. With movements. With textures. With comings and goings and dance steps and ice skating and outlandish flights of fancy and colors. With imagination. With the creativity that verisimilitude demands. With the inventiveness that necessarily leads us to the truth. The truth. Poor little thing, she, too, always waiting, always waiting in line to be discovered. Revealed. Made to shine before the wonder of her own light.

**211** But meanwhile back in Mexico, back at the airport and the alluring *güeras* already shining before the wonder of their own light, who showed the whole country the way of the light, back at the stretch between the glass doors and the car that awaited us, oh yes, that was what my new *compañero* said. He said: Let's go home.

**212** That house was the house of exile. Of exile within exile.

**213** And so we went. Of course we went.

**214** But I'm not going to go into detail here. Those details have to wait to be known, until the day I decide to write my memoirs or something. Because no one who practices the work of the word, either well or poorly, can resist the vulgarity of leaving behind their anecdotes, personal, intimate, any kind at all, in any form, for the  remembrance of generations to come, as though they were an indispensable font of knowledge for those ignoramuses, with no lives of their own, that comprise the majority of the inhabitants of planet Earth. Unless a premature death should impede it.

**215** Only a few facts, events, stand out. That year in Mexico I decided to have a son who, once we were back in California, turned out to be a daughter. I also met, in the third month of my pregnancy, a man. I worked on the editorial staff of a literary magazine: *La brújula en el bolsillo*. When the magazine turned one year old, the editor-in-chief decided to celebrate by publishing a special edition that would include blurbs of praise from the most distinguished writers currently living in Mexico, whether they were Mexican or not. And that was how, since I was in charge of soliciting all of their magical words, I had my oh-so-gratifying (and historical) telephone conversation with Octavio Paz. The man himself picked up the receiver on the second ring. I told him my name, which didn't mean anything to him, of course, and at once mentioned the magazine, which did mean something to him. Openly recognizing my Argentine accent, he made the pronouncement: "Look, why don't you stop fucking around up here? Why don't you get the hell out of my country, you and the rest of your political exiles, who only came here to fuck up our lives with your arrogance and your communist ideas, and take away Mexican jobs? That bullshit magazine is a commie rag. I won't have anything to do with it and I won't write any blurb. All you Argentines should get lost, go back to your country and clean up the fucking mess you left there. Get out of here! Go! Leave us in peace!" To which I, finding no better words amidst my emotions, and with no air in my lungs, said in short: "And instead of me going back to my country, why don't you, Sr. Paz, go back to the whore of a mother who bore you?" And hung up.

**216** Marks. Tattoos that seep down to the marrow of your bones. Blue arabesques etching themselves onto white marrow, final and irremediable.

**217** Life is transformed with each step. Days are molded, according to different emphases, accents, inscribed on our sensibilities, each instant.

Life is before exile and after exile. How much more affection and happiness would we have if we hadn't had the option of leaving our country. How many more genuine kisses. Friendly embraces. In solidarity. The tendernesses intensified in each gesture. Or maybe none at all, and in their place only a few profound, momentary looks of understanding.

And also, how many more times would we have died. With how much vehemence would our blood have been spilled, our contribution to an anemia of historic proportions. And who wants, who needs to die more times than we have already, with the death of each assassinated *compañero*.

**218** And that feeling of victory, of exercising a kind of power over my own body by recognizing that yes, my belly was going to alter certain paths, those old uncertain pathways, from here on out.

The great triumph over oneself. Over the organism

that one is. Over the vital pieces that constitute us and that, given a certain state of health, or sickness, or beauty, represent us. That represent the particular whims of our occasionally harmonious neurons.

**219** And so the bougainvillea. I mean: getting back to that arrival at the Mexico City International Airport: from that moment it was one year until I decided to return to Los Angeles.

And the bougainvillea. Cuernavaca. During the first three months of that year there were so many bougainvillea. Fuchsia, orange, red, and, every once in a while, white. Covering the fronts of the old colonial buildings. Falling, energetically, from the flat roofs of the boxy, whitewashed houses. Flustered, draped down the sides of the streets, stretched out, observing the movements of cars and passersby, open-mouthed, astonished. Just like I was. Just like I was, in the challenging task of understanding, of making some sense of the displacements, swivels, impulses, variations, undulations, and tremors caused by my new *compañero*'s existence, in relation to me, in relation to himself, to his daughter and to his parents. To the mother's dog and the father's parrot, intimate parts, both of them, of the familial group. Puzzling. Everything puzzling. And I say that, fearing that I'm mistaken, fearing that everything, in reality, was so - make that soooo - clear, that maybe it's worth it for me to make the effort to accept that life confronts you every so often with an enigma. And that attempting to elucidate those enigmas won't necessarily satisfy many curiosities. No. It may bring on an attack of spleen. Cardiac arrest. Unnecessary chronic pain. The kind that has happened to the desecrators of tombs, those who dared to reveal the great secrets, to unravel the great mysteries that humanity was hiding.

And all this among bougainvillea. Among *santarritas*, as they are called in Argentina. Those *santarritas* of my childhood before whose quiet, fuchsia memory I choke down my soup. Both soups: the tomato one with letters they forced me to eat at age four, and the vegetable one that I make myself eat now, to maintain my figure.

So now the dog and the parrot: they were as exiled as I was or, come to think of it, maybe less, but certainly more tangled up in the complexities of the family than I was. Because exile isn't just one thing. It's not a direct, simple phenomenon. It can't be expressed in linear terms by a pair of parallel lines. Nor by an elementary geometric figure like a rhombus, or a polyhedron. No. Exile is an uproar. A whirlwind of elements that aren't all recognizable. That fill the mind, stir it around, make it into a bloody brain shake. Let's imagine, now that we're on the subject, a kind of multi-colored marble, assuming that those involved believe that the brown terracotta of some privileged landowner runs through their veins, or perhaps the golden phosphorescence of the intellectual elite, or the blue blood of the national literary oligarchy. What a drama.

## 220

For that reason a separation can be providential. It clarifies the scenery. It dissipates the eclipses, the darkness. It restores lines and tones to the landscape. And changing cities? And moving from Cuernavaca to Mexico City? Great. That's what it's all about. Coexisting with musicians that play the same instruments you do. For an indefinite period, but one that's always new and musical.

And the pregnancy. And in the middle of the pregnancy that letter from Juliana. And David's attentiveness. And the writing. And the magazine. And the other Argentine exiles: their relationships, controversies, worries about their survival, about legality, their meetings and nighttime parties, their friendly gatherings, intellectual activities, their political discussions, their collective action, their certainties, their heap of doubts and questions. Their unnecessary excuses to keep human affection and the ties that bind alive. To weave together and consolidate a community that gave, on more than one occasion, the necessary answers.

**221** And that brilliance, that brilliant beating that occurs at certain points during the blood's circulation, suddenly, when we discover that the word we come up with is so appropriate to the page that we're writing, that it's nothing more nor less than the one, in pursuit of which, we were prepared to excavate, to scuba dive, to travel down into the very viscera of a volcano.

**222** And always, always accompanied (pursued) by the resonance, by the internal vibration, by the insistence of the simplest of questions: why? That kept me alive and expecting, interested and in a state of constant inquiry, so I don't get left without the fleeting, volatile answer. As if I didn't know it, as if we didn't all know it, by heart, since our own beginnings.

**223** And especially at this point, when I began to notice the appearance, on the way from itch to rash, slow but unmistakable, of an eye, about to open completely at around the height of my right clavicle.

There's now less and less of a chance of perceiving things only halfway. Fewer and fewer excuses.

And so, resigned to having to see, to having to take responsibility for the vision, the image that blazes before you, there's not much left to avoid nor much more to do than toss your head lightly backward, rest your neck on the edge of an armchair, and observe the ongoing spectacle of a world in motion. In silence. In silence because the sounds are legion and deafening, at times. Explosions, blows, laughter, gunshots, cries. Groans, snores, whispers, shouts of joy. The mewing, the murmur of water, the thunder in the sky, the music from within the bars, the mooing from the countryside, the death rattles, the expressiveness of orgasms. The grinding of tooth upon tooth, the croaking of the frogs against the water. And with eyes closed. Because the multiplicity of color is blinding. The rhythms. The thousand speeds. The needles sticking you in your veins, your eyelids closing, trains traveling on green. The intervention of light upon angles and time. The different brightnesses of different skin, their combinations and contrasts. The millions of hands shaking as one. The convulsive activity of hands against hands. The stubborn sparkling of the nighttime rains. The brilliance of the noonday sun. The irradiation, traceable yet hidden, of the blue of the newborn elephant's gaze. The deep red blood spreading out inside of a woman's liver as she's tortured. The tortured man's severed foot exhibited in that tree. The fields of tulips. The splendor of a diamond in a display case. The lazy violet of the afternoon. The confused quietude of Modigliani fed up with museums. You can see it all. And hear it. Without the intellectual mediation of the human effort to understand what's happening. You can see and hear it all.

**224** Let History await us. We're on our way. We're recovering the rhythm. Because if it isn't us, it'll be our children who catch up to her. The ones who will step on the train of her long black dress. The ones who manage to catch her by the neck. Who will force her to explain herself, make her clarify her reasons.

The unbridled one. The demented one. The one who pretends to be so innocent. Who's never there. Who's irreplaceable. The nervy one, the one who sold out. The unbearably open one. The stingy, arrogant one, uninhabited, empty, bursting with the shouts of phantoms, peevish, conceited, dirty, and traitorous. The liar. The unfathomable one. The withered one. The congested one, with the eternal flu. The delinquent. The one with fingers so soft and sure. The one without tongue or throat. The mute. The one who emits only shrieks. The damaged one.

**225** Because this also occasionally illustrious Lady travels at extremely high speeds, with free reins leaving phosphorescent streaks in the air behind her.

And having arrived at this point, when the itching finds its way to the most unlikely parts of your body, when it's no longer bothersome but longed for, since it represents three-dimensional sight, deep, hallucinatory, of everything that we've been given to see, we've already lost all fear. And the spectacle of the free, luminescent, multicolored reins against the absolute black of night, absorbs us. It hypnotizes us, drags us along, presses us into service, offering us no alternative. And if it isn't we ourselves that we're watching running behind the brilliance and jumbled color of that magnificent scene, then it's the children we love, who've made sense of our shouts. And our paleness. And the serenity inside us. And our shadow. And our ferocious desire for happiness. For contentment.

**226** And so here was the situation: exiled in a country that I intuitively grasped but didn't yet know, with the freedom to walk and to calculate that comes with not having a partner; surrounded by an abundance of friends and *compañeros*; without any money, because the magazine didn't pay jack shit; and with at least some mental clarity about the novel on its way, there was no other better project than a child. So with the decision made, I put my mind to the task. All that was left was to get my body in the game. And so when my period was four days late I finally knew for certain that two parallel events were closing in, having been conceived round about the same day: the novel that had been stuck in my brain like a hungry animal trapped in a burlap sack was beginning to be written. And the child, so often thought about and discussed with a certain close friend and with myself, had reached the dimensions of, oh let's say, a lentil.

**227** That's how opportunities usually incarnate over the course of our existence. Opportunities to take vengeance. To find the means to retaliate, feasibly and civilly. Call it payback, maybe not for the whole world, but at least for your home turf. But no. Madness of a certain scale demands compensation on a scale to match. Thus no outline, no completed manuscript, not even a published book setting the facts straight, would be enough. No child you could have, even one that could occupy that vital place abandoned by one of your many assassinated *compañeros*, would be sufficient. You would have to write so many books. You would have to bring so many children into the world. You would have to fill so many holes. You would have to have so much patience. You would have to gather each of the elements, every piece, each vindictive component, with such joy. With such humor. With such conviction that the battle needs us in order to be won. And nevertheless.

**228** And while you're composing the words, ordering them into paragraphs, assembling them into what one might call chapters, all the while imagining, calculating, the various odd forms that the fetus will take during one or another stage of the pregnancy (tadpole, alien, dragonfly, Venus flytrap, miniscule piranha, underdeveloped hippocampus, arabesque inflated with proteins, spoonful of rice pudding, spoonful of snot, anthill of activity, fluorescent light bulb, little piece of practically nothing, little piece of practically everything, shining pebble in the middle of the road, of the garbage dump, ricotta ravioli in tomato sauce, etc.) news starts to arrive. Bit by bit. From Madrid, from New York, from Sweden.

**229** The news from Madrid: Silvana Montes, ex-political prisoner from Argentina. Cuca to those of us who knew her best, now exiled in Madrid with her husband and two children (one three and the other one and a half) just left the hospital where she'd been admitted. They opened her and sewed her back up again without touching anything. The uterine cancer had metastasized beyond repair.

**230** From New York: Ignacio Suárez, known as Chivi to the boys in the Sierra Chica prison, died of a heart attack in the subway on his way to work. He was reading *The New York Times*. No wife. No children.

**231** And from Sweden: Leticia Flores Cardó, long-time veteran of Villa Devoto prison, exiled with her eleven year-old daughter, "disappeared" *compañero*, died a month ago of a brain cancer that had been removed twice.

**232** I don't need any more. Between these three pangs and my early pregnancy, chunks of vomit nearly reach the sidewalk across the street.

**233** You get on the *camión*, (bus, or *colectivo* as we say in Buenos Aires) sporting your new olive-on-a-toothpick look, a bus that traverses most of the city, speeding down Revolución and letting you out a few blocks from the magazine. You put one foot on the first step, the other on the second, pay, get your change, all the while employing a sideways strategy, so your belly bumps into fewer obstacles, your eyes darting back and forth searching for the shiny gold of a vacant seat. But no. Not one to be found. And the passengers who up until that moment hadn't been looking out the window, suddenly, coincidentally, find something terribly interesting to look at in the street. What could it be? Impossible to know. And the passengers who were looking out the window already, after a quick glance at the new passenger, especially the new passenger's belly, turn to look out into space. Others have found something on the soles of their shoes and so lower their eyes. The striking thing is that no one offers their seat. And since the trip is long and your arms, or at least one of your arms, is supporting all your weight, hanging tightly to the metal tube that runs the length of the bus, way up high, in a much too uncomfortable position, and there's no way to change positions (because, provided you're not on the verge of fainting, your pride wins out: there's no way you're going to go begging for a stupid, smelly little seat on a ramshackle bus that on top of everything never even gets you to the door of your destination), your imagination kicks in, becoming a very effective defense mechanism.

So let's see: let's give a name to the pot-bellied man with the gray mustache seated behind the old lady with the braids. Or no, let's not call him anything. There are times when names aren't necessary. What if, while I'm trying to recount the story of the mustachioed man who's pretending not to notice me so he won't have to give me his seat, I call him *Ovidio*? Doesn't work. Right? You have to find a way to keep it surreal. But don't go overboard. Because surreal surrealism or very surreal surrealism tends to irritate, in the heat of the moment. So why bother? Why spoil the possibility of the absurd, a possibility that so often leads to laughter, with such a violent jerk on the nut, the kind that usually ends up stripping the threads?

Let's say, then, that the pot-belly with the moustache saw my belly coming towards him from the back of the bus and, as soon as he noticed the disproportion of my proportions and rotundity of my roundness, the threat was clear to him. His lower eyelids darkened and the line that separates (or joins) his lips straightened from a benign curve into a tight, tense stretch, a line without margins where I could read more or less clearly Fuck off, you, don't think for a second I'm going to give my seat up for you, *güerita*, what did you do that got you that way, you gave it up didn't you, you little tramp, and when you did it, you enjoyed yourself, didn't you, well, so now you can just hang there, this bus is for people who work them- selves to death, not for people who fuck around. That's right, *güerita*, you just hold on tight to the back of that friendly seat, that won't let you down. It's all just a game to that fucking little squirt, a few goddamn jumps. And it's good for those arms of yours, they're way too skinny anyway. How did you manage to grab on to that big buck of yours, the one who left you that way, I mean, with such skinny little arms. Or was it some stud who grabbed on to you. So you just hold on, *güera*, tight, 'cause no one's going to give you a seat. A working man like me isn't going to take a chance standing up on this bus, especially after the shit I went through last night, because I really got shit- faced, and with the fucking hangover I've got I wouldn't give up my seat for my own mother, the old cow, my moth- er the saint, who may be a saint, but I'd like to know, or maybe I wouldn't really like to know, how it was that the old bull fucked her so that I came into this world, the old whore, I wonder if she enjoyed herself, probably not, saints don't enjoy themselves, of course not, my mother the saint, who thinks she's the Virgin Mary now and who has the right to kick me out of my own fucking house, that I built up brick by brick, that's mine and no one else's, fucking old bag, forgive me, dear Lord for the sin of telling the plain truth, who chased me out with a broom this morning because I slapped my fucking old lady around, the mother of my child, I hit her with an empty beer bottle, worthless bitch, who can't give me any more sons, who can't get pregnant, God knows why, even though she's still young, and I picked up that bottle and I told her that I was going to go stay with the other one, the one who's a real load or whatever they say, but who's ten years younger and fucks harder, she gets up on me and she bounces, do you hear me, and doesn't stop, shaking like she's going to have some kind of breakdown. She's the one who'll give me more sons, you'll see, I told her, and hit her big old blockhead with that bottle and next thing I know here comes all this blood, red everywhere, splattering over everything, and so here comes Old Lady Saint with her broom and throws me out, kicks me out of my own house, the saint. So, fucking *güera*, don't even think I'm going to give you my seat, I'm tired, way too tired, and I'm not getting off yet, not yet I'm not getting off, *güera*, 'cause I don't even know where I'm going, it's not so easy to know where you're going, where these buses will take you, the buses in this city, your woman, your women, where the mother who brought you into this world will send you, in this fucked up fucking world, where, now you know, fucking *güera*, there's nowhere to sit down, where there's never enough to go around, where there's never anything worth having, nothing *güerita*, not even a little goddamn seat.

**234** That's why you get off the bus and you feel your belly button itching. And, through your dress, you manage, though only partially, to scratch it. And now inside the magazine building, anxious, you head straight for the bathroom for a variety of reasons: one, the deep need to observe the bulb, object of various itches and scratches. Another, the joy of being able to take advantage of such a unique opportunity: pregnancy gives you the right to occupy the bathroom as often and as long as you like. So that, comfortably seated – seated at last, after an epic three-block walk from the exhausting odyssey of the bus to the lyrical sound of urine on water – in the stall, with your dress hiked up, with the bulk of your belly six months along, various blue veins crossing your skin this way and that in a desperate search for a non-existent waistline, no longer a symbol, a metaphor, or a form of metonymy because nothing comes close, within this rigidity, to movement or anything like it, yet something is working its way out. In the very place that it itches and itches. In the spot where I scratch and scratch, instead of going and sitting down at my desk and trying to figure out what work I've left undone since yesterday. In the place where I scratch and scratch I discover, with my own imprudent, determined, substantial happiness, another new eye opening up. Really, I mean it: opening up.

**235** The brightness hesitates but not in an anguished way, it doesn't hold onto anything, it doesn't hang, and its kingdom is the magnitude of its own essence. It disperses, it expands, it makes itself disappear, restoring itself at every point where it left itself behind. It enters and leaves its own world, everyone's world, everything's world, and shows off its vanity with the grace of a bourgeoisie heroine. It persists, flaunts its achievements, and receives applause, its gaze sweeping back and forth in the self-satisfied manner of the victorious taking stock of the spoils that strength, success and power have provided. Free, hiding neither satisfaction nor brilliant whiteness. For there is no shame, nor blame, there are no fears nor too many desires. She is moderately immoderate, and she knows it, and celebrates it. There is no way to capture her. She can do without her public, at any rate. She works alone, distantly regarding the public. But if they were to disappear, she would continue on, ensconced in her own vastness.

What would happen to the balance of things if so much brightness were confined to remote, austere, places, if it were sent to deal with the basest of shadows, with certain daybreaks of exile, also sometimes alarmingly white? What if she were made to experience the bewilderment of such contrasts, and the perplexity of multiple, unexpected similarities?

**236** Certainty, conspiracy, ceremony, tannery of the past. The tannery of the past that exists only as the present. Water gushing from the everyday faucet making the future closer to today, to the river of today, bringing with it all that will enter our bodies and pass through them, giving us a future, a present and whatever past is running around in circles out there, jumping up and down at our feet. Biting our ankles, leaving rashes that no amount of repellent can prevent. Tanned hides, old hides, brushed anew each day.

**237** The edge of the leaves, of those leaves, so given over to the task of confusing me with their barely perceptible vibrations, through the shadowed glass of the window that interposes itself, forcing me to keep my distance. The edge of those lanceolate leaves and their tenuousness. Their weightlessness. And the drowsiness that begins to half-close my eyelids (though of course they always recover their strength). The ones on my face, the ones on my knees, all, absolutely all my eyelids.

**238** Under the sun, indelicately laid out in both body and mind, and as free from clothing as was permissible at the time,

I make my most transcendent decisions. You'd have to see exactly what entered my veins, what rush of temperature activated what glands and what secretions in such a way that my most intimate beliefs, settled in corners, connected to the production of life, defined themselves in action. Shaped themselves into letters. Into words.

You'd have to see.

The planets spin around us so many times, they engrave so many circles and curlicues and spirals and springs within their bounds. So many spins. So many journeys softened by a circularity that dizzies us imperceptibly, that cradles us, that puts us to sleep. And all of it behind our backs. All of it, I mean all, without having consulted us. Without having kept us in mind. And you, in the middle of a customary doze, tossing and turning inside the cave of your own stupidity trying to keep an antenna sensitive. A neuron unanesthetized. An eye, one of so many, half-open. So much ruckus, so much fighting to keep from losing even one miserable part of the spectacle. To hold on to the vibrations of remembrance. The signs of memory. In you. In yourself. In your own body. The most wretched remnants, tracks left by the events, bricks used in the construction of History. So much effort. Fuck. And the sun, directing it all from his throne. Without granting us any right to reciprocate. To brighten his domain a bit, to add to his eternity. Alas, we're condemned to receive.

And so, opened to the point that the blocked and unconscious molecules that make me up (poor innocents dizzied by the merry-go-round of their own alienation) allow me to be, open to the sun, laid out in my bra beneath the powerful, warm light that desiccates the balcony – whose solid railings, I should clarify, shield me from the eyes of the neighborhood – my perspective of my surroundings interrupted by that mountain, soon to be an erupting volcano, that is my seven-month belly, I decide that my son, who I'll name Carlos Ernesto (and let the discerning guess why I chose those names and not others), will be born in California.

**239** Meaning you have to get a move on, take a shower, get dressed, go see the man that you're interested in at the moment (not necessarily the one who helped to engender the little insect), relay your irreversible decision, find money for a ticket, pack your bags and fly to Los Angeles.

**240** And so, as I said before: how can you express the appropriate gratitude for so much generosity? To the sun, I mean. A card. Ah, I don't know, maybe a bunch of poppies. Tulips. Or sunflowers, that will always admire him face to face. Hug him a little. Kiss him on the mouth. On the neck. A small yet significant, conspiring smile offered from the little, covered balcony of your days. From the telephone. From my conversation with David about whether he'll be home so I can see him right away. From the Mexican shower. From this bus where, I swear to god, there's not one goddamn little seat free, empty, vacant, condescending, so help me, *güerita*. I swear to you.

**241** So, baby, take a bus on the wild side!

**242** And you'll have to put on your roller skates and produce, amidst the rubbing and shaking of the elements, an accident, an explosion. Some display of energy. Some event.

**243** And since we human beings are a disquieting chain of insolence, treachery, loyalty, obsequiousness, safe conduct toward what sounds like liberty, of prolegomena and foolishness, of stupidity and arbitrariness, of disobedience and tenderness, of obedience and hallucination, of pathologies and cruelties, of ignorance and surprising understanding and solidarity, of a wealth of knowledge and of inconceivable idiocy, besides so many other attributes, it wouldn't be a bad idea to sit down for a while and think. Beneath the sun or beneath the plump darkness that persists in presaging the next storm. To think.

And even though we know that absolutes don't exist and that everything is a question of degree, and since the composition of the human race is so remarkably complex and, despite the conspicuous presence of many people of humor, intelligence, sweetness, creative ingenuity, understanding, courage, common sense, healthy madness, selflessness and great intentions, the delinquents among us tend to stand out, the state terrorists, the dissatisfied, the genocidal, the depraved, the vulgar and the irresponsible, toward the end of April, 1982, two years before the facts of this story were about to transpire, the inexplicable Falkland Islands War inserted itself into the lives of the Argentines living in Argentina, and among the other two and a half million spread across the globe. And in the middle of all the racket and the gigantic lies being told about the outrageous destruction of adolescent bodies, the war suddenly ended seventy-two days later, with the surrender of the military dictators, genocidal by vocation, and the handing over of the islands to the British, all wrapped up in cellophane with a golden bow on top. For that reason the delinquents running the country had to hold democratic elections and resign their posts – not their power – to other less murderous inepts. And so now, in December, 1983 some anxious and curious exiles from different corners or not-corners of the globe began to look for ways to get a little closer and take a peek at what was happening. Events on roller skates, events that left bright red marks on the oh-so-delicate parts of History's body. Poor thing. Poor little mistreated thing. And David was one of them. So we said good-bye at the airport in Mexico City. That airport I'd arrived at with the premonition that, even though I'd bought an enormous chocolate almond ice-cream cone, I was going to eat another very small one, this one (bland) vanilla.

And six days after that farewell, I returned to that same airport for my own trip, my return, with a tourist visa, to Los Angeles, and shortly thereafter a leap to Santa Barbara where not exactly Carlos Ernesto was born, not precisely the one with the famous namesakes, but instead the infinitesimal, gracious, enthusiastic Sara Julia.

**244** Oh, the misfortune of a name. Symptom and synopsis. Silence and dark, empty cavern. The named: that malleable collection of tissues, the sacrificial object.

**245** One night before the event (because the night before always holds the key to the facts to come) my friend Jim placed me at the center of the crime scene with a question he was pondering. Here is, if not verbatim, then roundly and approximately, what he said: Beautiful, little city, Santa Barbara. So many hills, you know? So much gossip, so many people on bicycles. So many breakfasts at seven in the morning along the Pacific coast, wrapped up, covered by the mist of early spring, of the still imperceptible spring. Gorgeous. Gorgeous. So many poets, painters and

visionaries, all struggling in the throes of so much rich-
ness. Do you feel OK? Doesn't writing, when you're about
to give birth, divert your attention? By that I mean, the
attention your little boy might need? Or little girl. You
know, I was thinking: what if it's a girl? I don't want to
contradict you of course. I know you're going to have a
boy and the pictures of Marx and Che that Daniella and I
hung up for you in your bedroom show that we trust your
intuition, since it's always been right. But, what if it fails
you this time? Why don't you, just for fun, nothing serious, you know, think about a - oh I don't know - a name,
or two perhaps, a tentative idea for a girl's name? How
about it? Because I mean you're so ready to give birth,
you probably won't last another day. And what if it's a
girl and there you are, in the hospital, bewildered by the
turn of events, not knowing, in the middle of all the pains
and the contractions, what name to give her?

**246**  Without knowing how to predetermine
her. How to sketch out the path for her.
How to narrow her freedom. How to
condemn her.

**247**  *Pasos bajo el agua*, that still enjoyed
the absence of a title and that was, also,
nine months old, was inundated by
women. All of them, poor things, on predetermined paths,
with destinies, with definitions, with labels and names.
And in prison. In a way I'd managed to shake loose from
my shoulders, from my shoulder-blades, from my lungs,
the tradition of conventional paternity, so it occurred to
me, and I had fun with the idea (though in a few seconds
I'd throw it away) of recording this birth with my last
name alone. And so spare whomever it was emerging from

my loins the disgust, the disagreements, the weight on their conscience of having to hate their progenitor. And not just that: with such a clear path ahead, one so open and clean before their eyes, they could choose their own stigma and stick to it, and thereby be responsible for themselves and their own madness. They could hand down their own sentence. Or, in any case, bestow on themselves the great luxury of deciding who they might be, whom they might be in the future, and be truly themselves, in complete control of their own selves. To give themselves, let's say their wholly proper name. It also crossed my mind – and I found it even funnier – through the thick walls of my cranium, like an arrow ignited by all possible flames, to record that human being without any last name at all. And without a first name. With nothing. Offering them the possibility of complete happiness. With that arrow, of course, the fury of impossibility crossed my mind as well. And of paradox.

But okay. Going through the manuscript pages of *Pasos*, looking for a sentence, for a title for the being who ended up being my daughter, I got stuck on a group of four letters that, at any rate, sounded round, brief, and clear. And that group, to clarify a little, represented me throughout the book, represented many other women, and represented all the women contained in my existence. But my friend Jim insisted that I would feel safer if I were protected by two granite masses. One wasn't enough. We would all feel more tranquil, more secure, when we were faced with the explosion that was coming a couple of hours from now. And then Julia, the incomparable offering that Vanessa Redgrave made to that great interpretation of the world, eager for events advancing on skates over the rutted road, from a *Pentimento* infinitely unfolded, came the second, trembling designation.

**248** You try. You do the best you can. You speak, make certain gestures, modify your tone, raise your voice and begin to think that the people destined to receive so much expressiveness are deaf. Because nowhere are there any signs that the messages have been received. You observe no reactions, nor any comprehension. And the sending of the message, the decisiveness and preparation it requires, the successive attempts, the frustration at your failure, and the subsequent recuperation and recovery of resolve required to begin again, steals away so much time. They suck out your energies, energies that can only be replaced through the imagination. Lucky for you imagination is a vocation you've been cultivating.

**249** And for that reason, because of all the time required for these efforts, big and small, not to mention the medium-sized, that lack the adrenaline of the big and the impact of the small, or vice-versa, because of the massages and the caresses that are needed for the restorations and the nights and days that are necessary for the reconditionings, let the battle wait for us. Because we're out of here already. We're way gone.

**250** There exists a certain people, a certain race of the well-intentioned and a certain implicit ineffectiveness apparently inherent to well-intentionedness. Certain dietary deficiencies, perhaps some irresponsible lack of protein that results in damage to their vision, and promotes blindness.

**251** So, now that we have, together in the same place, both the one trying to reconstruct herself and the other one, the well-intentioned one, ready to contribute the happy ending to the series of facts that are to follow, the contradictions begin to peek out, right in your face.

We might describe the scene this way: a political exile, nine months pregnant, thirty years old and with sufficient mental clarity to, in spite of the nearness of the birth and her sensitivity to the written word, shows, makes visible, a strength that hadn't been less noticeable before, before exile, in prison, nor in her relationships with her family and friends. That's one side of it. On the other, her friends (from California, a proper couple, adequately appointed according to the canon of conservative good manners, at least as far as one can see from the far side of the line that divides the domain of the relationship, let's say a more than acceptable economic situation), so excited about shiny little gunked-up eyes, the button of a snotty nose and the hairy little ears of a living thing they could already see peeking out from between my legs, a couple having serious problems conceiving their own child. In other words, no children and no possibility of having one in sight. Clearly ready to help find a good hospital, a reliable doctor and a place to live (theirs) for the exiled friend just arrived from Mexico with a belly about to burst.

The exile (and friend) – who could perceive a growing desire, more and more clearly expressed, by the well-intentioned couple to, as both of them were part of the commotion surrounding the coming of this being into the world, participate in the spectacle of birth – began to suspect that a misunderstanding was starting to grow.

No, no, no, said the exile. I'll have none of it. A birth isn't, if the one at the center of it doesn't want it to be, a television program, or anything that needs to be shared. Let's not allow this kind of confusion to get started. This act of opening my legs and pushing out this child is totally private; I don't even know how I'll bear having the doctor and nurse around.

But, why? Went the pleading, worried inquiry of the well-intentioned couple. Why? We're a part of this, and we're so happy about the new baby's arrival. We almost consider it our own. Besides you're alone in this situation.

The exile, whose face was turning successive shades of red, later yellow, then green, reminded her Californian friends that this "you're alone" was the happy result of one of the best decisions she'd made (under the imposing Mexican sun) in her life and that she wasn't, not on your life, going to change her mind either now or ever. And, besides, no kind of company could add to the already fabulous adventure of having a child, especially not at its very beginning, the birth, the unrepeatable, irreversible, singular and terribly private event of birth.

But listen, said her friends, this is not an experience that a person should go through alone, without ready affection at hand. Not only did you decide not to include a father in your plans, but your own parents are back in Argentina. Don't pretend to be superhumanly strong. It's as if you have no concept of being an exile, far from your people, without your family and about to have a fatherless child. What's wrong with you?

Look, answered the exile pointedly. I don't understand why you've decided to distort reality this way. You're telling me I don't know what it means to be exiled? Far from this and that? You're telling me I don't know what it means to have a child alone? I'm asking you, see if you can satisfy my curiosity: Have you two experienced anything on that list that makes you worry about me so much? Do you two have an idea what it's like to be far from friends, the dead and the disappeared, the living and your family, as difficult as that relationship might have been? Shit! Did you ever have a child, with or without a father? I can understand, only rationally and only partially. The idea you have stuck in your mind is that this country, the country where you were born and bred, is the best country in the world, and you can't get over the idea that the inhabitants of the rest of the world are savages and barbarians. I can sort of understand that because ignorance, which is the most frightful of human ills, goes in all directions. But I'm not going to let you even try to convince me that a weakness, a helplessness, a lack of conviction about my own decisions that doesn't exist now and didn't exist before, exists. Don't treat me like a poor imbecile dragged around by the winds of circumstance, because when you do, I start to see you as insensitive, omnipotent, handicapped, and insolent, swimming in a sea of blindness and optical illusions. If you need someone to protect, to care for and dedicate yourselves to, to spoon-feed, to make into a victim, my child and I are the worst candidates for the job. It's a bad idea: don't even go there. I will not repeat this: I don't want anyone in the delivery room. I don't need anyone. I deplore the idea of someone there who isn't the child, the doctor and me, and if you keep insisting I'll go to another hospital, with other doctors, and you'll never see me again. And I mean never. How is it possible to understand that when you repeat and repeat that you love me and respect me, you pass so lightly over my person, as if I didn't exist? So please, don't make me be the bad guy responding to your demonstration of good will, that in reality has all been a misunderstanding, a lack of deference, a lack of respect for my desires, my needs and my ways of doing things. Let's just say: it's a shame.

Oh, please, said the couple in unison, please, please, don't take it like that. Calm down. Calm down or you're going to make the baby nervous. Don't rush the birth. If you're going to take it like that, even though the last thing we want is to abandon you in this difficult moment, it's OK, we'll leave you in peace. But we're going to be taking care of you, watching over you from where you can't see us. Subtly. Without making you more nervous or bothered. Enough already, with what you have to deal with, having this baby by yourself.

The exile felt the ever-growing fury peering out between her tongue and the roof of her mouth. She felt that all the eyes, that were already covering even the least likely places in her body (though, to tell the truth, it never ceases to be a wonderment to be able to see everything from such surprising angles) were mobilizing and blinking together. You could almost say that they were demonstrating a distinct tendency to trespass across the boundaries that kept them in their place, that until now hadn't allowed them to complete their leap. There was no room in the exile's body for so much indignation. She didn't understand how it was possible to make the effort necessary to resist such sanctioned stupidity. The pressure couldn't fit inside. Making space would have meant eliminating some of the elements that were already taking up so much space, elements that had ceased entering, ceased sitting there comfortably, ceased giving me that pleasurable feeling.


252     But you can't allow yourself the extravagance of exploding, bursting, bleeding dry from hate. Better to decompress. You have to invent a valve so you can let the trapped air escape, the air that bubbles up in those hidden corners where your bones and muscles, your muscles and veins, your cartilage and fatty tissue, your blood vessels and tendons, come together and attach, since none of them

have any reasonable access to the outside. And so, once again, like so many other times, who or what has more control over these kinds of situations than the imagination? Or memory. Because it's not fair, either, to pretend that the only thing the sacred valve could come up with would be made-up things. No. It would also be nourished by memories. And by the distortions and the traps and the dirty tricks that reminiscence uses to make us pay our dues for each time we deny reality, each time we boycott our self or our idea or our project; each self-defeating act, each slip of the tongue. Each time we back down. Each renunciation. Each panic attack. Each retreat before the swaggerings of the things that oppose us. Each form that our defense mechanisms take, that are apt to confuse. That can get themselves mixed up with our ethical armor. That kill so wantonly. Memories that reappear through the colorless openings of nostalgia, through the crusty and rusted shutters of what we've lived.

And *that* Jim and *that* Daniella, the ones from back then appear, spontaneously hospitable, wanting to know all the humorous details and to share the joys when possible. Who seemed to understand. Or who understood. *That* Daniella who filled, up to the top and with all kinds of foam, a bathtub at the end of each day, so that I could surrender all my exhaustion, my knotted muscles, the shooting pains in my neck, the shouts inside me drowning in my guts, to the lapidary effects of the bath salts. *That* Daniella who showed me the deserted parts of the Santa Barbara hills with crystal-clear explosions of laughter, who during our many hikes photographed the baby sheep around us: sheep? I don't know. Those babies covered in whorls of white, incapable of fleeing our intrusion. So many Daniellas. So many lovely Daniellas, back then. Her lively topaz eyes that broke into an infinity of lights with each word she said or heard.

And Jim, Jim in his tiny, enchanting cabin, surrounded by his lawn and his untamed plants out back, struggling, Jim, with words, secluded in his wooden nest with little, creaking windows. Fighting with words, accepting them, letting them beat him, avoiding their significance. Relinquishing to them the responsibility for taking charge, entering or leaving without having been called upon. Letting go of their hand, abandoning them to luck, which so often is neither luck nor destiny. Jim in his cabin behind the house. Jim and Daniella: a refreshing breeze. A favorable wind.

**253** You two promise me, then, said the exile, in the hospital, between contraction and curse, that you're not coming into the delivery room? Right? Of course, her friends replied. Of course. We've already talked about this enough. It's your decision. Not ours, yours. It's what you've decided, and we'll respect it to the letter. Don't worry about it anymore. Concentrate on doing the best you can. Try to relax and concentrate on the baby. We're leaving. We're going to the waiting room. The nurse said that she'll go find us and tell us how everything went and give us your room number. OK? Everything will be fine. Bye. We'll see you in a little while. Let me give you a kiss. Be strong. We love you.

Phew! The exile breathed freely, seeing them disappear down the corridor in a hurry, as if rushed along by something, making a concerted effort not to bother her anymore. Of course. There are times when your mind can mix everything up. Who knows what change in the functioning of your hormones, your chemicals, who knows what chemicals, it must be something about the titanic effort of birth that could be making me so defensive. They understand. Even though it's a little hard for them and even though they insist, they understand my overriding need for privacy. My pressing need to embrace the length, the magnitude of this birth by myself, only by myself. Of course they understand. They've always been a wind in my favor. There's no reason for a change. Now more than ever. She breathed again for a few seconds before confronting the volcanic onslaught of a new contraction. Seconds during which two nurses helped her to fall heavily on the gurney to be transported to the delivery room. Shit, shit, shit, she shouted through the corridors on the way to the culmination of a nine-month event. *Mierda*, she spit out, bilingual and without moderation. Who was the creative son of a bitch who invented this son of a bitch, unfair and disgusting way to bring a child into this son of a bitch world. Tell me who the jerk was. Bring him to me and I'll beat the shit out of him. I swear to God I'll beat the shit out of him.

And so it was that two large doors parted and the gurney passed through into the delivery room. Where the exile didn't see much, wide walls, green maybe, lights on the ceiling perhaps, some metal shapes, that also a maybe. And all expectant and dressed in green smocks and white masks that covered their noses and mouths, four people all in a row facing the door through which she was entering (on roller skates, certainly): the doctor, a nurse and those two voracious Californian friends Jim and Daniella. Jim outfitted with a black camera and its very busy flash. All while the pain became worse than anything ever before, all while from among the folds of her recently shaved crotch the fuzzy head of the miniscule event began to emerge. All while she heard the doctor say *she's* beautiful.

**254** Would that History not fly to those rhythms. Would that it tried to slow down. Come down a little, come closer to us. Allow us to mount the broom. Share it.

**255** Because an unshared broom, a broom seldom ridden, doesn't do its job. It loses its hair. It atrophies. Becomes sterile. Stops sweeping. And transporting. And shining. It takes off more slowly each time. With less impetus. And performs more lamentably each time. More pathetically. Filling you with sadness and rage.

**256** A couple of suitcases and a basket. In the suitcases a few books, the indispensable ones. And clothing. In the basket, a three and a half month-old baby girl. Aerolíneas Argentinas. By boat in a huge container, many hundreds more books. All thanks to the financial support of the United Nations. Headed for Buenos Aires, after four stretched out, shrunken years. It's not true that it's not possible to define them.

**257** You enter and you leave, you go and you return, surprisingly, unenlightenedly, at times; endowed, with the requisite shadows, with indispensable spaces of light between shadow and shadow. You carry with you your acquired patrimony, accumulated, instant by instant, of insomnias, of questions, of outbursts of laughter in the middle of the night, of self-accusations, of the vaguely sinister forms of forgetfulness, of excessive memory, that opens a path between your musculature and the creaking complaints from your bones. With one finger of one hand, perhaps against an unknown wall, maybe against the bluish bark of a tree that's also unknown to you, you invent a support. And lean on it. Or you believe that you're leaning. Or you know that you're not leaning, because nothing could support you in the midst of all that shaking, but imagining that there's a support there helps you to find the real one.

There's no beginning and no end to the speculative caravan of investigation, of the search for the word, the one that draws, outlines, though it be weak and feverish, the name of the facts. No end to the tracking of the profound understandings about what happens to us each day, the sounding out of the reasons for laughter, for estrangement, for the piercing invention that is long-distance pain. There is no end because there was no beginning, or at least we didn't detect its initial signs. Didn't we detect the initial signs? Slightly? Since when were we so far away? At what vulnerable point of our ancestry did we create the distance, and begin to feel, or not to feel, distant?

Where are we from? How did we get here?

It's possible, four years into a barely breathable childhood in Rosario, to half-open our short thighs that weigh on the sides of the white toilet that supports us (somewhat, always somewhat) and observe ourselves and judge ourselves from the confines of our physiological, anthropological, ontological realities, to separate our legs as we feel the tickling of urine on its way to hitting the water, resounding, it's possible, I mean, to suppose that you urinate like no one else urinates. It's possible to suppose, and even have no doubt whatsoever, that the noise of your own urine is not replicable. It's possible to forget to dry yourself and to run with your panties around your ankles expressing your anguish, the definitive loneliness of unknown origin experienced in the instant in which the disparities and the discords of the future have already been defined, have already been pinpointed. To run in desperation from the bathroom to the kitchen between chokes and coughs to share with supposed motherly wisdom the discovery that there is a certain knowledge, something we already know, that can be seen in your urine, perceived in the sound of urine against water, about yourself. And it's possible to be halted by a frightfully present shout, so present, it reminds us above all that decorum and decency rule: you had better pull up your panties.

And it's possible, more than twenty years later, to sit down on a toilet on the other side of the world, ensconced in curious latitudes, in strange hemispheres, to close your eyes, it's possible, and repeat the old thought that early on confirmed the distances, the extensions, the differences, to corroborate it, love it. And hate it, of course, when without even having dried the rest of your legendary urine with toilet paper, you glanced around in a circle, half circle, at a bathroom full of strangeness, and noticed (your hands trembling, your pulse suspended in the midst of your decision as to whether it's better to come to a permanent crashing stop or to speed up with equally lethal acceleration, a moan flowering between your frozen teeth and your confirmed suspicions: I knew it, I knew it, I told everyone, that so much development, the First World and that whole pack of lies; and the crossroads created between the rags of light and the raveled threads of shadow that attack between the opaline glass and the wide window, suddenly irrecoverable) that there is no bidet. What a blow to your consciousness: you've noticed, audience absent and present, the absence. The absence of a bidet in your country of exile. And since an absence is always highlighted against the backdrop of contrast, of comparison, let us repeat, that while we wash our hands, the image of the ever-present, reliable and shiny (or peeling

and full of rust) Argentine bidet in the bathroom of the
house where you grew up. Or the houses. Or the place
that you rented. Or the bathroom in that bar. Café.
Service station. And your brain keeps going, no one can
stop it, the inevitable destination: prison. The prison
bathroom. In the prisons. Where it's not possible, in spite
of our selectively creative memory to remember, to bring
back any memory better than the present sight. No bidet,
no toilet: a latrine. An anatomically appropriate hole,
ready to unload our private waste, many of our habits
and some of our sobrieties. And vanities. And different
prides.

Thus, exile takes its intermediate place somewhere
between prison and freedom. There's always a system of
measurement. Some parameter. Some outline of a smile.
The longitude between the bidet and the toilet, between
the toilet and the latrine, between the latrine and the
bidet, that ungraspable Pythagorean theorem, maybe
irresolvable, has just been proposed.

You enter exile before you leave your own country,
when you're thrown out, displaced, expelled. And with
exile stamped on your back you leave it: displaced by your
own desire for reunion. For kisses. For all those kisses we
hope for from all that has the ability to kiss: the trees that
were just planted back then. The half-built buildings. The
tenacity of some of the winds, that cover our entire body
with kisses. The heat of January with or without ice
cream. The chairs in the café. But I mean, not all of them:
only the ones that insist on keeping one leg shorter than
the others. The screeching made by the wheels of the train,
that also kisses, I don't know what, maybe the rails, but it
kisses, especially as it gets farther away, relentlessly, as it
sinks into the inflammations of the air.

Such that you return to your country of origin. The
first, the archetypal, that was the scenery for your first
measurements, comparisons, starting point of every going

away. You return. You come back (partly) to investigate the truth of an idea that circulates among most exiles which posits that the return to one's country marks the end of a stage in one's life called exile. You return, therefore, to your friends, to the ones who stayed alive, trapped between the walls of systematic, obligatory hiding. You return, not without the requisite resentments, to your parents, who now have a four month-old granddaughter. And just as you return to them you repel off of them, confirming the spaces, measurements, and vast distances in between. You go back, maybe with a little more conviction, to the streets of Buenos Aires. You return, for a while, to the man who still occupies (not all of) your attention. You visit your old birthplace, Rosario. You sit down, in a café. Alone. Without the baby. Dressed discreetly, inconspicuously, trying to pass unnoticed. With a book that serves as your refuge while you make more or less furtive glances around you. What did you bring to read? You didn't just bring any old thing that was lying around. No. Nothing can be left to chance, ever. With perfect care you considered the relative merits of each title. The possible consequences of each content. Because if your shelter should prove too simple, it wouldn't exert enough attraction to keep you tied to it at the very moment you were relying on it to lower your gaze, making the effect as real as possible, and distracting from the calculated nature of your performance, even though it was going to be obvious anyway. And if it proved to be too difficult, that just-described situation, where you have to pretend not to notice, and where, on top of everything, you're nervous, emotional and sweating, you wouldn't be able to concentrate totally on the printed word.

Meaning: what's needed is a book of, shall we say, intermediate complexity. Which is precisely the kind you don't have and wouldn't want to own. And besides and most importantly: it's one you wouldn't dare be seen with.

Those cafés after all are the ones you used to hang out in, where you used to live, where you took exams, wrote poems, read them to your friends, debated the philosophies of the Revolution. Your friends who survived must still be going there. So explicit is the rhythm that's stamped into my blood. How warm the saliva that flows down the curves of my throat.

And so with the book open on the café table (nothing more nor less than the first volume of *Ulysses*, to the page on which the adjective *snotgreen* is used to describe the color of the sea, shaming every writer on Earth for not putting more creative energy into their work) I order a tea. Without milk, without sugar and without lemon. The waiter and his moustache are the same as they were five, ten years ago. I know that. I don't say anything. He tells me I look familiar. And I smile repressing my desire to tell him my story. Three young men arrive. They sit down at the table beside mine. They're younger than I am. Now please: there are people who sound like adults who are younger than I am. They order coffee. They talk, a lot. Loudly. Very loudly. To be heard by I don't know who. By themselves, it seems. No one speaks in loud voices like that if they don't need to hear themselves talk. One of them, the one with the shrillest voice, says he just got back from a work trip to Tucumán. He says that everything is so beautiful there. That since the military bombed it a few years ago and annihilated three towns of sugar cane workers everything is calm and orderly. That the streets are resplendent, clean, he says, the streets of San Miguel always lined with orange trees. And suddenly there's no book worth a damn. There's no author simple or complex enough to distract me from such a theatrical display. No Joyce who could attract me or manage to absorb the smallest neuron of my days.

My friends, the ones who are still alive, don't show up. Where are their hands, the ones that clung to the warmth of their coffee cups in an effort to find the irrefutable. The noble. Where do they prop up their elbows, now missing, exerting no force on the edges of this dark, unpolished table covered with traces. Who is now fortunate enough to feel that involuntary brush of shoe against shoe, as the person across from you excitedly blurts out some idea. Where is the idea. Where is the coffee. Where is the outburst of laughter at some absurd argument. Where is the surprise and the anger at the solemnity and fear. Where is the strength of the concept, the force of the judgment, the clarity of the reflection. Where is the construction of the archetype. The sustaining of the paradigm. The development of the obsession. Upon what surface do their fingers drum now, against what faces does the smoke of successive unfiltered Particulares dance. On the basis of what axiom will I hear my assertion refuted that it is healthy to write in cafés where your friends gather because missing your friends while you work in your own house doesn't help your productivity and being interrupted by their arrivals keeps your blood pulsing and without blood you can't write. Maybe there's no axiom, judging by the silence of the entryway. Where can I find that equation, that brilliant line, except inside my own lungs.

Maybe they don't come here anymore. Maybe none of that comes here anymore. And my tea is cold. And it has no sugar. Nor milk. Nor lemon. And I'm exiled from exile, where I could drive fifteen minutes so I could sink my gaze into that groove that's both formed and washed away at the same time between the clotting of the sky and the bubbling of the Pacific.

Where do I come from, how far do I get, how do I draw nearer to what. Move away from what.

How am I going to fix everything so I can survive the sadness, the arrogance, the paralysis, the violence. The constant cry of those who, tortured, are made to keep on coexisting with their torturer. With their hangman. How to absorb the signals, the signs of horror splashed on the walls, the façades of the buildings. Between the cracks of the bas-reliefs, of the meticulously joined moldings around the windows. The traces of blood, the leftover sweat, the particles clinging to the shadows, that reveal that a human head, maybe young or old or tremblingly childlike has been smashed against the porous cement that remains exposed. How to discriminate among the diversity of signs. How to digest the message without exploding constantly in vomit and choking. How to live together with the assassin without feeling like an accomplice. How to coexist with the martial rhythm, that reverberates through the streets, unpunished and commonplace, where the hostility that lives between memory and forgetfulness deploys its plots, nets, traps, that populate the inescapable places of pain.

Where during the hottest time of the afternoon in January 1985, in an ice-cream parlor on the Buenos Aires avenue of Corrientes as I shared tiny portions of a strawberry ice-cream with my almost one year-old daughter with the burning air interrupting any attempt to breathe, a woman with her two colorful scoops approached to ask me what kind of cruel mother I was since I was sure to give my little daughter laryngitis. Her behavior justified by the fact that she was a nurse from the Children's Hospital, which sanctioned her intrusion into my life and authorized her insults. How I would have loved to have had the nerve to tell her that just two days before I'd taken my daughter to the Children's Hospital for her shots, and why didn't she spend more time promoting proper hospital hygiene there, since the place was hopelessly buried under a grimy layer of dust. Inside and out. That same hospital was filled with the shouts of a mother whose child had just received the wrong vaccine. A nurse, the author of the deed. Not the same one with the ice-

cream probably but another one just like her. But no. I
didn't have sufficient dictatorial power. At least not
enough to overcome hers. So I resigned myself, or didn't
resign myself, to explaining to her, with few words and
less patience, that if she didn't stop saying such stupid
things I was going to stick the ice-cream cone up her ass.
Hers not ours, clearly. After which she disappeared from
the ice-cream parlor protecting her ice-cream cone, herself from her ice-cream cone, hurrying off to other ice-
cream parlors to protect other children from guaranteed
laryngitis.

What's the problem with me and my country. Where
are the symbols. I look for the gestures that once guided
me, the characters that ignited and energized the road I'd
used to get closer to myself. I search for the great
metaphor, the gigantic word that translated the meaning
of life for me. But there isn't one. There are no more, it
seems. Or at least what is there is inaccessible to me. It's
hiding from me. It seems to want to, I don't know, tease
me. Where am I. I don't know where I am. Right here,
and I have less doubt about this than the savior nurse
might have about all the laryngitis in the world, I am not.
I am not here.

Could it be that exile, that one, is now other exiles
besides? Could it be that the first exile is going to repro-
duce, unfolding like an accordion, like a succession of
mirrors connected at their edges? Could it be that from
now on the primary exile, the one needed to save my life,
will be repeated in others infinitely, without limits, without jokes, without doubts and without alternatives?
Could it be that there is no going back from exile? Could
it be that I've been transformed into some kind of traveling exile? Concave? Convex? Centrifugal? Centripetal?
Concentric? Paracentric? Interior exile inside exterior
exile, like the layers of the onion, a doll within another
Russian doll, such is my exile? All the exiles? Bone cells,

nerve endings, red and black corpuscles, blue and purple, translucent and covered with opacities, my exile. Bark, cackle and secretion of humors and hormones. Marks of millions of feet on my skin plugging up my pores. Dryness and humidity on the inside of my nose. Of my bone cavities. Wise urine, plagued by immutable ignorance, rooted in my own bladder. Romp in the air, spring of time, extending to the four infinite winds, infinite sword hacking off the base of my stomach, the entrails of the earth, unequivocal burning, unmistakable, never removable, inflammation in the vocal cords, a droplet appearing in one eye, what some would call a tear, a converging, moistening, astringent dripping. Permanence. Argument with inclement weather. Establishment of certain joys. Fight against flower, tree and need. Sweet and juicy summer peach, exile. Surprising and unavoidable encounter between your teeth and the pit. A peach pit that needs no adjectives.

Here where I was born, where I was who I am, where I left and where I have returned, I am not. Here where I work to survive, where I write, where I raise my daughter, where I love in some way a man, where my first novel is about to be published, where I eat, where my daughter eats, where I urinate with that particular sound of my own urine, where I gather with my friends, the old friends who've managed to elude death, my new friends, I am not. Nor am I, nor am I, nor am I, let me clarify, walking along the festooned shores of the ocean, pressing down with the soles of my feet, playing at leaving some ineffective footprint on the moist, warm sand of the beaches that give shape to the western edge of the spread-out city of Los Angeles.

And what do you have to do to be where you are. What do you do to let your mind follow your body or to keep your body from resisting the actions your mind wants to take. To arrive where you are, finally. And to be able to stay there. So that the brain might finally arrive where the body is and wait for it. What. How. To clench your fists. To dig your nails into the palms of your hands while holding your breath. To remain. To stay. To bind the mind to the body. To tie it. Stick it with glue. But no, that doesn't work on the moist parts of your body. OK, then: wires. Stitches with wire. Would that they held. Would that they kept the mind and the body in their respective places. That would avoid diversification. Dissolution. What are their respective places. What space belongs just to them. What is space, what is place. What does it mean that something belongs to a location.

How can we manage to be complete where we are. Who establishes where we really are. Who decides where we should be. Who said that the function of the mind is to control the madness of the body. Who thinks that it would be catastrophic if the body didn't obey the commands of the mind. Who insists that harmony is necessary. Which is the necessary harmony. Are we dismembered, we who have our right foot in Madison, our left hand in Lusaka, our right pinky in Cairo, our liver in New York, our nose in Buenos Aires, our thighs in Barcelona and our digestive tract in Los Angeles?

What is not being dismembered. How can you understand the concept. For example: Fernando, not dismembered, was born in Argentina in the city of Córdoba. He was raised there and there went to elementary and high school. He went to the University of Córdoba. He studied geography and got his degree in three years. He liked his profession. He got serious about it. It wasn't hard for him, in no time he'd finished his studies and gotten a job in the department where he'd studied. He had opportunities to travel in America, even in Europe and Africa but that didn't excite him. Maybe he talked too much in geographical terms about all the countries of the world. To students in his class, to himself at home. The result was that at the age of 48 he'd never left Argentina. He didn't leave for the rest of his life. He never left, really. But he had, this much is true, a wife who was a high school History teacher and three children, two of them teenagers. A stable financial situation, not too many friends but enough so he had a place to go or visitors on Saturday night. He also went to the movies once in a while on Sunday with the whole, or almost the whole, family. He didn't have his lungs in Stockholm, his right shoulder in Sidney, an eye in Vienna or his forehead in Tokyo. He had all his members in Córdoba: the members of his body, the members of his family, the members of his thoughts and ideas. Nothing related to him crossed the borders of the city of Córdoba. Fernando was, and remained, whole. Or at least all his parts were assembled in such a way as to allow him to feel whole. Perhaps blind people also enjoy the benefit of a kind of interior solidity that, if we knew it, we who have been filled with unasked-for eyes might learn to envy.

Nevertheless I keep asking myself: what is not being dismembered. What is cohesion. Who are, where are those who enjoy such genuine solidity.

**258** With your nose (and maybe also with a knee) in Buenos Aires, one day that first novel gets published and presentations are organized and you're leaving one of them when you notice two guys with dark, short hair waiting for you, wearing sunglasses at night and leather jackets and jeans. To tell you, to give you a message, a text whose author they were clearly in agreement with: Come here, they say. Come here 'cause we've got a couple little things to say to you. And listen good: Who do you think you are? How dare you come back to this country and publish this pack of lies? We're going to make you shit your pants, bitch.

Get out of here and take your daughter with you, because if you don't watch out we'll make you both shit your pants. And be happy that we're warning you. Four years fucking around here is enough. This isn't your country. Make no mistake. This is a country for patriots. Take care you don't ignore us, that is if you don't want us take care of you.

And then they walk away with the slowness of someone who knows what he's saying. Or one who thinks he does. Or one who knows nothing but hides his ignorance pretty well. I don't think I'll wait around trying to figure out the difference.

**259** You enter and you leave. You hold up the world with one hand and with the other wipe away the uncertainties and doubts that this same world scratches on our bodies. You open and close your eyes depending on the direction and the intensity of the winds that blow, irretrievable, in this hemisphere that shelters us. You take a half step forward with staggering movements and smiles of justification and then take four steps backward. You gather your strength and take a leap that's worth ten steps and then as your adrenaline level goes back down you go back two and the tempered joy strengthens you for the next battle. We enter into laughter and we leave it as if we were experts on the subject of when to laugh and when to restrain yourself in that uncomfortable, confused, vague grimace. You breathe in and hold the air in your lungs, alternately, as if holding the lights inside you, the brightnesses, the winks that come together and disperse to one side or the other in the expanding atmosphere. And you release the air feeling the loss of the light and the coming of the shadows and the phantoms that lie in wait for you and sometimes don't. You begin to wail creating no small amount of racket and you open a path in your grief, through its boiling, lava-like contents until you leave it behind vanquished, annihilated. The wailing vanquished, its battle lost, and a kind of overwhelming calm. You enter with your arms outstretched like a sleepwalker, with your sleepwalker arms outstretched, emerging from a hallucinatory series of questionings, of questions, of attempts at answers. You abandon the different fires with your back in flames and you run, you run, fleeing all that fire, fanning it with your desperation, making it full, adding in the details, the intensities, and you devote your strongest impulses to it. The eyes on your neck, on your elbows, on your two knees and the other ones that have always been there below your forehead have been damaged, that's for sure. But that's why you have eyelids, trembling, stirred by emotion, quick to the rescue, moving up or down slowly as if distracted and deaf. You leap away from the path, you enjoy the fresh mud of its edges free from pavement or plants and you learn to nose around, carrying phobias and other loathsome things on your back, among the decomposing, putrid cadavers of birds suddenly stopped in flight, among the deer, among cats caught by surprise. And you get back to walking on the flattened, hot gray of the asphalt with almost the same vigor, with almost as much fervor as the evening before. You manage to leave behind one labyrinth, another, and another, and proceed to the next as if there were nothing else besides labyrinths, as if labyrinths were the only way to live. With their winding ways. With their corners and traps. And you move through them, dizzy, guided by the hypnosis of your days, trying with some effort to endure the effects of those few lucid glimpses that, inevitably, rescue us from one labyrinth and move us on to the next. You enter in a state of exile, you abandon it and you settle yourself on the one waiting for you the next moment, and you stuff your holes with exiles and more exiles the way they used to stuff old cushions with wool, old dolls with burlap and you feed on them because what doesn't kill you makes your life longer, nourishes it and if we try hard enough even makes it bit more beautiful.

With one hand you hold up the world and with the other you begin to push in the white ends of the bones poking out of the openings, wounds inflicted over the years of history, of the succession and the accumulation. You enter into the events, you leave them slipping along on skates of different kinds: the kind that save us; the kind that can't distinguish between a smooth path and one that's been spattered with rocks and nails; the kind that have learned to get around the risks and move forward at the usual speed, a few inches off the ground. History doesn't wait. She only sits down to rest from her running around looking back, distracted, already moving again, not interested in whether or not we catch up or if the distance between her and those who want to play a leading role in it grows larger by the minute. Absent, she follows her own rhythm.

And since what hasn't killed us nourishes us and sustains us, it becomes life itself. In its allergies, its fibroses, its asthmatic whistles and in its laughter overflowing around the edges of what we are day-to-day. Of our daily travels. On roller skates or barefoot, the soles of our feet getting tougher and smelling more and more like trampled pasture, mud, pebbles and tar. Like the song you go along humming. Because you certainly sing, you certainly intone one melody or another and make up some new ones, every once in a while a new one, watching the vermilion leaves of fall, sticking a little branch into an ant hill on the corner, spitting out the bitter taste of the night, adding an accent to destroy the diphthong, discovering a new little mark on the living room wall, lamenting the loss of an earring, pondering the need to comprehend a logarithm, waiting for the dye that reddens your gray hair to take effect, looking intrepidly for a book that, how could it be, where did I put it, pulling out that hair with a tweezers that, try as you might, will not give up, playing by ear on the keys of someone else's piano, soaking your feet in salt water, counting your toes over and over, observing the nails, cutting them, tidying them, filing them, doing those things that take your toenails back to what they once were: smooth, soft, rounded. Touching, squeezing, twisting the bone of your bunion, as if to reassure yourself that they're there, solid, the bunion, the toes, as if to prove that there's no doubt, that yes it's possible to count on their painful presence, that they're there, that they're the final piece and support of the body that makes you up, that defines you. That they won't fail to come to your aid in any kind of emergency that might require running, or escape, a chaotic dance or one in a more classical style or a long relaxing walk or a hurried one or a leap: adored feet, your own, mythical bunions that transport you from one edge of the cliff to the other while your eyes with all their skills instruct you as to the swells, inform you about the voracities, train you in what stirs below the air, in what shivers, writhes, boils in the depths of that abyss that the elasticity of the old, renovated springs saves us from. Intimate, private ballistas shared so many times.

As we go along recreating, reinventing the leap. The pirouette. Acrobatics. In the center of balance. At the intersection of the coordinates that pinpoint, at once, silence and shrillness. The point where the air elects to be immortal.

# About the Translator

Clare Sullivan is a teacher and translator who lives in Louisville, Kentucky. A faculty member in the Classical and Modern Languages Department of the University of Louisville, she earned her Ph.D. in Spanish from New York University in 2001.

# About the Author

**B**orn in Rosario, Argentina, in 1953, Alicia Kozameh had just finished her undergraduate degree at the Universidad Nacional de Rosario when she was detained as a political prisoner. The military dictatorship held her from September 1975 to December 1978. For the first year of her imprisonment, she was held in the infamous Sótano ("basement") of Rosario's Police Headquarters. Afterwards, until her release in December 1978, she was held captive in the Villa Devoto Prison in Buenos Aires. On parole until July 1979, she fled Argentina for exile in Los Angeles, California, then Mexico City, where she edited a literary magazine and worked for a news agency, then once again moved back to California. She returned to Argentina for four years, 1984-1988, where she continued her studies in Philosophy and Literature at the Universidad Nacional de Buenos Aires. After the publication of the first edition of her novel *Pasos bajo el agua* in 1987, Alicia was threatened again by political repression, so she returned with her four-year-old daughter to Los Angeles, where she founded Monóculo Literary Workshops, a series of creative writing workshops. Since 2000, she has taught creative writing and English literature at Emeritus College, a division of Santa Monica College.

Kozameh's first published novel was *Pasos bajo el agua* (Buenos Aires: Contrapunto, 1987), translated as *Steps Under Water* by David E. Davis (Univ. of California Press, 1996). Her 1989 novel, *Patas de avestruz (Ostrich Legs)* was translated into German by Erna Pfeiffer and published as *Straussenbeine* (Vienna: Milena Verlag, 1996). In 1999, *Pasos bajo el agua* was published in Germany as *Schritte unter Wasser*, again translated by

Pfeiffer. Her novel, *259 saltos, uno inmortal* was published in Cordoba, Argentina, by Narvaja, 2001. Alción Editora published a new edition of *Pasos bajo el agua* in 2002. *Patas de avestruz* (2003) and *Ofrenda de propia piel* (2004) were also published by Alción.

Excerpts from her novels have been published in various anthologies, including *AMORica Latina* and *Torturada*, both in German, and in *Redes de la memoria* in Spanish. Excerpts from *259 saltos* have been published in English in *Southwest Review* and *Miriam's Daughters: Jewish Latin American Women Poets*. She is the author of many short stories, for which she has won prizes, including the *Crisis* Best Short Story Award and the Memoria Histórica de las Mujeres en América Latina y el Caribe 2000 Literary Award. Kozameh has given readings and lectures around the world, and has worked extensively with Amnesty International to share her prison experiences and to promote human rights.

# About the Author of the Introduction

Gwendolyn Díaz was born and raised in Buenos Aires, Argentina. She received her Ph.D. from the University of Texas. She studied with Jorge Luis Borges and Carlos Fuentes, among other notable Latin American authors. Díaz is a Professor of Literature in the English Department of St. Mary's University in San Antonio, Texas, where she also serves as Director of the Graduate Literature and Language Program. Díaz has published three books, *Paginas de Marta Lynch* (Celtia: Buenos Aires, 1985), *La palabra en vilo: La Narrativa de Luisa Valenzuela* (Cuarto Propio: Santiago, Chile, 1996), and *Luisa Valenzuela sin máscara* (Buenos Aires, Feminaria, 2002). Her fourth book, *Women and Power in Argentine Fiction (1950-2005)*, will be published in 2006 by the University of Texas Press. Díaz is a co-founder of the Latina Letters Conference. Díaz has spoken in conferences in Europe, Latin America and the United States and has served on the Executive Committee of the South Central Modern Language Association. Her awards include a Fulbright Grant, a Carnegie Mellon Postdoctoral Fellowship, the St. Mary's University Distinguished Professor Award and an Honorary Professorship from the Universidad Católica Argentina.

Wings Press was founded in 1975 by Joanie Whitebird and Joseph F. Lomax, both deceased, as "an informal association of artists and cultural mythologists dedicated to the preservation of the literature of the nation of Texas." The publisher/editor since 1995, Bryce Milligan is honored to carry on and expand that mission to include the finest in American writing, without commercial considerations clouding the choice to publish or not to publish. Technically a "for profit" press, Wings receives only occasional underwriting from individuals and institutions who wish to support our vision. For this we are very grateful.

Wings Press attempts to produce multicultural books, chapbooks, CDs, DVDs and broadsides that, we hope, enlighten the human spirit and enliven the mind. Everyone ever associated with Wings has been or is a writer, and we know well that writing is a transformational art form capable of changing the world, primarily by allowing us to glimpse something of each other's souls. Good writing is innovative, insightful, and interesting. But most of all it is honest.

Likewise, Wings Press is committed to the treating the planet itself as a partner. Thus the press uses as much recycled material as possible, from the paper on which the books are printed to the boxes in which they are shipped.

Associate editor Robert Bonazzi is also an old hand in the small press world. Bonazzi was the editor / publisher of Latitudes Press (1966-2000). Bonazzi and Milligan share a commitment to independent publishing and have collaborated on numerous projects over the past 25 years.

As Robert Dana wrote in *Against the Grain*, "Small press publishing is personal publishing. In essence, it's a matter of personal vision, personal taste and courage, and personal friendships." Welcome to our world.

*Colophon*

This first edition of *259 Leaps, the Last Immortal*, by Alicia Kozameh, has been printed on 70 pound paper containing fifty percent recycled fiber. Titles have been set in Cochin type; the text was set in a contemporary version of Classic Bodoni. This font was originally designed by 18th century Italian punchcutter and typographer, Giambattista Bodoni, press director for the Duke of Parma. All Wings Press books are designed and produced by Bryce Milligan.

Other recent works of
Latina / Latino fiction and poetry
from Wings Press:

*Among the Angels of Memory /*
*Entre los ángeles de la memoria*
by Marjorie Agosín

*Psst ... I Have Something to Tell You, Mi Amor*
by Ana Castillo

*Drive: The First Quartet*
by Lorna Dee Cervantes

*Casi toda la música / Almost All The Music*
by Ángel González

*Frieze* (volume six of the collected works)
by Cecile Pineda

*Indio Trails: A Xicano Odyssey*
*Through Indian Country*
by raúlrsalinas

*Sonnets and Salsa* (2nd edition)
by Carmen Tafolla

*Baby Coyote and the Old Woman /*
*El Coyotito y la viejita* (2nd edition)
by Carmen Tafolla